Praise for Kate

"Perry's storytelling skills just keep getting better and better!"

—Romantic Times Book Reviews

"Can't wait for the next in this series...simply great reading. Another winner by this amazing author."

—Romance Reviews Magazine

"Exciting and simply terrific."

—Romancereviews.com

"Kate Perry is on my auto buy list."

—Night Owl Romance

"A winning and entertaining combination of humor and pathos."

—Booklist

Other Titles by Kate Perry

The Laurel Heights Series:

Perfect for You

Close to You

Return to You

Looking for You

Dream of You

Sweet on You

Tamed by You

The Family and Love Series:

Project Date

Playing Doctor

Playing for Keeps

Project Daddy

The Guardians of Destiny Series:

Marked by Passion

Chosen by Desire

Tempted by Fate

Sweet on You

Kate Perry

Phoenix Rising Enterprise, Inc.

© 2012 by Phoenix Rising Enterprises, Inc.
Cover Graphic © Corbis Photography - Veer
Interior Graphics © Magdalena Kucova - iStockPhoto.com

This is a work of fiction. Names, characters, places, and incidents are products of the author's imagination or are used fictiously and are not to be construed as real. Any resemblance to actual events, locales, organizations, or persons, living or dead, is entirely coincidental.

Shout Outs To...

...the places that cheerfully gave me a place to sit while I worked on this book:

- ❤ *Contraband,*
- ❤ *The Brew,*
- ❤ *Rapha,*
- ❤ *The Grove (on Chestnut),*
- ❤ *and, most especially, Nectar.*

...my posse, Martha White and Parisa Zolfaghari. They helped make this book a reality instead of a vague notion about cake and Batman.

...YOU. Without your love and support, I'd be scooping French fries at McDonald's. I'm thankful for you every day.

...and, lastly, my Magic Man, because he tells me how great I am every day, and he means it. I'm sweet on you, baby, in case you couldn't tell.

Chapter One

*D*ANIELA LAY ON the cold tile of Ground for Thought's kitchen and contemplated her life. It was, in short, a mess.

Her grandmother used to tell her there was a recipe for everything. If her grandmother were still alive, she'd say this was no different. Nonna would tell her she needed to taste the ingredients of her life and figure out the right balance of flavors.

In this case, the ingredients were one slight Italian woman, a full serving of hot blood, a dash of stubbornness, all spiced with a talent for cooking—plus a liberal dose of unhappiness.

It just added up to a bitter dish.

The kitchen's swinging door creaked open. "Daniela? Are you still in here?"

Caught. She sighed. She'd hoped for more alone time. "Yes."

The confident clacking of heels sounded on the tiles, and then her friend Eve was standing over her, peering down. "I thought you came back here to make a private phone call. What are you doing lying on the floor?"

"Thinking."

"My kitchen floor is better for thinking than yours?"

"Your kitchen is nicer." It was smaller than hers, but it was finished and homey. There was the lingering scent of vanilla and sugar, and it reminded her of baking with Nonna. It also didn't have construction going on, a nosy assistant hovering close by, or telephones ringing nonstop. "It's peaceful here."

Eve stared down at her, hands on her hips. Then she kicked off her shoes and sat cross-legged next to Daniela. "Want to talk about it?"

"No." She shook her head. It should have been uncomfortable on the stone tile, but her mass of curly hair provided good cushioning.

"Do you want to bake something? Baking always makes me feel better, especially when I do it with a friend."

"*Hell no.*" Unable to stay stationary, she popped

up to sitting and faced Eve. "Can I make a confession?"

"Of course."

"I haven't baked in months."

Eve's pretty face scrunched up. "You baked the cake for my wedding a few weeks ago."

"That's the only thing I've baked since the summer." It'd been a labor of love, because Eve was the only one who'd treated her like a person instead of a commodity.

Daniela frowned at her new friend. "Why is that, anyway?"

"Why is what?"

"That you treat me like I'm a real person."

"Have you been sniffing powdered sugar?" She put a hand on Daniela's forehead. "You feel warm. Maybe you're feverish. Maybe I should call Marley."

"Don't threaten me. I don't want to talk about my traitor-of-an-assistant." She pursed her lips. "Or the man formerly known as my brother. Tony is dead to me."

Grinning, Eve shook her head. "You're so Italian sometimes."

"I know. I'm a walking stereotype."

"But you own it and make it work for you." Eve

tucked her hair behind her ear. "So tell me about your brother."

"I told you already. He's dead to me. If my grandmother were still alive, I'd ask her how to curse him. Nonna had the evil eye."

"He must have seriously upset you to make you want to put the evil eye on him."

Seriously upset didn't begin to cover it. "For my birthday, he had his secretary send me flowers."

"That's nice, isn't it?" Eve asked carefully.

"No, it's not. The card read *Best Regards for Another Year*." She paused meaningfully. "That was it. It wasn't signed or anything."

"Oh."

"And it was my thirty-fifth birthday." Eyes narrowed, she pointed a finger at Eve. "Everyone says thirty is awful, but it's thirty-five that smacks you upside the head."

"Should I worry that you just cursed me?"

"It's nature's curse." She slumped. "It hit me hard, and Tony didn't even have the decency to call me to see how I was doing. I ate take-out Chinese food at my coffee table in the living room as I watched TV. It was pathetic. *I* was pathetic."

Sweet on You

"There wasn't anyone else you could have spent the day with?"

"No. These days, people like me for what I do, not who I am. I've become all fame and no substance." She threw her hands in the air. "What have I done with my life? I bake cookies for spoiled, rich people."

"But you love to bake." Eve frowned. "Don't you?"

"I used to. Now I'm not sure. I've become a brand instead of a person. Even my own brother sees me as a dollar sign." That was what upset her most, because Tony had once been her best friend.

Eve touched her arm. "Have you told him you're upset?"

"No. I'm sulking at the moment." Daniela stuck her lip out just a little more to show her pique.

"Yes, you are."

"It's very satisfying."

Eve laughed. "In the long run, you should say something to your brother. Otherwise, he won't know he did something wrong."

"That's the problem. I'm afraid I'll tell him and he still won't realize he did something wrong." She shook her head sadly and stood up, brushing off the back of her jeans. "I appreciate the talk though. And the use of your kitchen floor."

Laughing, Eve stood up and hugged her. "My kitchen wouldn't exist if it weren't for you. You're welcome to use the floor, and anything else, whenever you like."

That thing in her chest that had been tight for so many months loosened a tiny bit in the warmth of Eve's friendship, and she squeezed her new friend tighter. "Maybe moving to San Francisco wasn't complete insanity."

"San Francisco is never a bad idea, and moving to Laurel Heights was serendipity." Eve linked an arm through hers and walked her out. "We take care of our own."

The community was why she'd impulsively decided to move. She'd done a booksigning at Grounds for Thought and had fallen in love with the neighborhood. Eve had introduced her to her women friends, all professionals but, more importantly, all welcoming and nice. Plus, Laurel Heights had seemed like the ideal place to open a West Coast flagship kitchen.

Though finishing the remodel hadn't been high on her priority list lately.

"Want a biscotti for the road?" Eve asked.

Sweet on You

"No." Turning down biscotti was a true testament to her state of mind. She loved biscotti, especially Eve's. They weren't like her nonna's, but they were a close second. "I think I'm going to go for a walk."

"Good decision." Eve gave her another hug. "I'm having a girls' night at my place next week. Will you come?"

She hesitated. She'd never been the kind of woman to have many girlfriends. She'd had her brother growing up, and then she'd been focused on her career. Women chefs were few and far between, and the few she knew were more competitive than friendly. "I'll think about it."

"Let me rephrase my statement," she said, holding Daniela's arm. "You *are* coming. Bring champagne."

Shaking her head, Daniela walked out of the café, marveling at how smart Eve was to make going to her girls' night so easy. Maybe she'd actually go.

Thinking about it, about her brother, and about the career she was beginning to hate, she walked up Sacramento, past Fillmore, not caring that the hill was steep. People complained about San Francisco's hills, but she loved them. Walking up one made her feel like she'd accomplished something.

God knew she hadn't done much lately. She'd been avoiding making decisions on everything and, consequently, everything was on hold—catering gigs, interviews, appearances... And then there was the remodel on her new boutique outlet in San Francisco. She'd managed to convince Tony that it was a good idea to open a West Coast office, but the construction wasn't done yet.

It was her fault. She'd been dragging her feet on making decisions. Now, the wolves were closing in.

Well—*wolf*, singular. Her brother. He'd been pressing her to get off her butt and make things happen.

Antonio Rossi wasn't her favorite person right now. How could you be too busy to wish your beloved younger sister happy birthday? Granted, her parents hadn't called either that day, but they'd had an excuse: they'd been somewhere in India and had called as soon as they could.

Daniela looked around and realized she'd walked all the way downtown. With a shrug, she kept walking, all the way to the Embarcadero and the Ferry Building.

She loved the Ferry Building. It was a place to

Sweet on You

indulge all your senses. She walked through the vendors slowly, watching the people, smelling the spices in the air, looking at all the food. Normally she'd have spent hours milling about through the shops. Today she walked through the building to the piers outside.

A movement by one of the Dumpsters caught her attention. Too vigorous to be a rat, she blinked in surprise when she saw it was a boy.

His hair was scraggly and sticking up in various places. He wore jeans that were too big, bunched a little at the waist. His T-shirt stuck out from the bottom of his oversized hoodie. In his hand, he held half a baguette that he'd obviously scrounged out of the Dumpster.

Her heart sank. She reached for her purse to pull out some money to give him for food but realized she hadn't brought a purse.

Then he pulled out a ragged stuffed animal. Tucking it in his sweatshirt, he picked up the small store of food he'd harvested from the garbage and walked away, furtively looking around like he was worried about being caught.

The food she understood—he was obviously hungry—but the stuffed animal perplexed her. She

Kate Perry

guessed he was twelve or thirteen. He was in that gangly, awkward phase that happened right before adolescence. The last thing a boy going through puberty would want was a pink teddy bear.

So she did the obvious: she followed him.

She took care not to alert him that she was on his tail. She bet he'd lose her in the blink of an eye.

Clinging to shadows, she followed him all the way to a dilapidated building South of Market.

It was condemned, based on the heavy chains and padlock on the front doors. Just in case there was doubt, there were signs posted all over in addition to the yellow Do Not Enter tape.

She studied the building. It looked like an old motel, boarded up and forbidding, with broken windows, graffiti, and padlocks on the doors. The only spot of lightness was the east side, which was covered in Dali-esque murals spanning from the ground all the way to the roof. Close to the sidewalk, there was a *For Sale* sign, as if someone would willingly buy this dump.

What was the boy doing here? She watched him carefully wiggle his way into the building through a jagged window.

Curious, worried, she followed him in. Fortunately, she wasn't that much bigger than he was, otherwise she'd have had trouble getting in.

She didn't have to go far to find him. She followed the sound of young voices. She peeked around the corner just in time to see him hand the pink bear to a little girl who had cowlicky hair just like his.

The girl gasped, her eyes widening when she saw the toy. She took it carefully. "For me?"

"Duh." Grinning, the boy ruffled her hair.

She grasped it, staring at it incredulously. Then she grabbed the boy in a huge hug. "Thanks, Jimmy."

He patted her back awkwardly.

A woman called out from somewhere down the hall. "Jimmy, are you back? Did you find food?"

"Yeah, mom," he yelled, taking the girl, who was obviously his sister, with him as he hurried down the hall.

Daniela stood there and watched them disappear, the echo of their voices fading. She looked around at the building. Trash littered the hall, and the smell of urine assaulted her with every inhale. She flipped a light switch on the wall next to her but nothing hap-

Kate Perry

pened.

They lived *here*?

She felt guilt over being so unhappy when she had so much. She had a large house in Laurel Heights, a four-story monstrosity that Tony had arranged for her to rent, as well as her flat in New York and *pied à terre* in Paris. She'd never known hunger, much less been without her own bed to sleep in. They were so different than the pampered kids she was hired to bake cakes for.

She wondered if either the boy or girl had ever had a birthday cake.

Her heart broke, remembering the way Nonna used to sit her on the counter in the kitchen as she baked cannoli or made pasta. Daniela had learned about life and love sitting on that counter. Without that, she had no idea where she'd be right now.

That boy had to scrounge for food to take home to his sister. Her brother would have done that for her. He used to protect her from bullies who teased her about her big, alien eyes, help her when she didn't understand math, and threaten to beat up any guy who broke her heart.

Once upon a time.

Sweet on You

She walked down the hall. If someone bought the building, that poor family would be out on the streets, most likely.

Turning the corner, she wondered where she was. This wasn't the way she'd entered. Disoriented, she looked around, trying to figure out where she'd come from. Shrugging, she pushed open the swinging door in front of her to see if there was an exit.

No exit—just an industrial-grade kitchen.

Of course, it was completely trashed. Careful not to brush up against the appliances, all caked in grime, she made a pass through, looking at the space with a professional's eye.

To make it functional, it'd have to be gutted and power-hosed. But the walk-ins were of good quality, and the range just needed to be cleaned. The space was open and would accommodate a large crew serving many people.

With one last slow turn, she went back out the way she came, fumbling down the hallway until she found her way out.

At the sidewalk, something made her turn around and look at the building again, and the sale sign caught her attention.

The building, with its enormous kitchen, would make a great soup kitchen.

Daniela studied the building with fresh eyes. There were a lot of homeless downtown—you couldn't ask for a better location. She imagined a fully running kitchen, cooks bustling to serve the hungry.

She imagined baking for people who genuinely appreciated her baking. For people who cared more about the food than the cachet of having her cook for them.

It was a *brilliant* idea.

Feeling a rush of purpose for the first time in forever, she hurried to the street and hailed a cab. "Sacramento and Laurel," she told the driver as she climbed in. "Hurry."

Chapter Two

Nico Cruz stood in the living room window of his suite and gazed out at all of downtown San Francisco below him. He should have been listening to what his second-in-command, Jason Lethem, was saying about the deal they were closing, but instead he stared at the Christmas lights and decorations cluttering Union Square and the surrounding streets.

Bah humbug.

Of all the holidays, Christmas was his least favorite. It reminded him of everything he'd lost and underscored that, as much as he'd regained—as far up in the world as he'd come—some things were beyond his reach.

Like happiness.

As much as he acquired, as great as he grew his empire, it wasn't enough. He had anything he could possibly want. Fancy cars. Private jet. He lived in the

Kate Perry

Mandarin Oriental, for chrissakes.

He looked at his reflection in the glass. He was average height, broad in the shoulders, wearing a handmade suit that cost as much as most families made in a month. His expensive watch peeked out from his sleeve, and his hair was the kind of perfect that only a two-hundred dollar cut could buy.

It just wasn't enough. He was still unsatisfied and, to his own eyes, he still looked like the street thug he'd been as a teenager.

If he went to a shrink, he'd be told that he'd been so starved as a child that he overcompensated now. That he'd never be satisfied, because it'd never be enough. That he'd never be able to shake his gangland roots, because he wasn't ready to forgive himself.

The shrink would be right. There was no reason to waste the money to prove it.

"And I hired elves for the holiday season," Jason said loudly.

Frowning, Nico turned around. "Excuse me?"

Jason gave him the flat stare that intimidated other businessmen.

Tugging his sleeves down, he strode to the table

where Jason had laid out all the contracts and sat down. "Did you think I wasn't paying attention?"

"It certainly looked that way," his right hand said in his crisp British voice.

When he'd first hired Jason twelve years before, Nico had been impressed with the man's business mind, but he'd hired him for his elegance. It softened his own rough edges to have someone so cultured in his corner.

Because underneath the silk shirts and hand-stitched shoes, he was still the street thug that he'd been as a kid. The edges may have smoothed out a little, but they hadn't been sanded away completely. Given the right circumstance, he could be just as ruthless as he'd been living on the street.

It made real estate the perfect milieu for him.

Jason set the papers aside and steepled his hands in front of him. "Nico, you've been more aloof than even you usually are. You've taken brooding to a whole new level."

"I'm not brooding."

"Aren't you?"

"No," he said, shutting that conversation down before Jason started psychoanalyzing him. Jason

Kate Perry

enjoyed dissecting Nico's "inner workings," as he called them.

"Is it a woman?" his right hand asked.

Nico couldn't fault Jason's relentlessness. That was one of the reasons he'd hired the man. But his personal life was personal—and nonexistent at the moment, except for the occasional casual date. He was too busy conquering the world. "Just finish what you were saying, Jason."

"Before you started to daydream about sugar plums, or your woman *du jour*"—Jason gave him an arched look—"I was saying Parsons was ready to close the deal. There's still a bit of negotiation, I think, but we're close."

"Good." He checked his watch. "Anything else?"

"Yes, since I have your attention now." He shuffled some papers until he found what he was looking for. Holding them out, he said, "The dilapidated building South of Market you've wanted forever was just put up for sale. That old motel."

Nico stilled. Then he took the pages from Jason.

The MLS listing detailed the usual information: square footage, number of units, and asking price. It didn't say that the building had been a flophouse that'd housed countless poor families. That the gangs in the Mission had recruited their foot soldiers directly from those barren rooms. That people had died there.

Like his brother Eddie.

He swallowed thickly as he looked at the photo of the edifice's front courtyard, where he'd found Eddie's body dumped, like it was trash. There was no evidence of the murder, but he still saw the blood pooling on the pavement.

He'd been waiting for this building to come up for sale for twenty years, so he could buy and raze it until not a speck of it existed. But the owner had adamantly held on to it, even after it'd been condemned in the '89 Loma Prieta earthquake.

"What changed the owner's mind about selling?" Nico asked hoarsely.

"Death. His heir wasn't as averse to selling it as the original owner was. There's just one catch," Jason warned.

"What?"

"Someone else expressed a strong interest in the building."

He calmed. He always won. "That's not a problem then. Make sure you outbid him."

"Her." Jason shifted through more papers until he found what he was looking for. "Daniela Rossi, the world-renowned pastry chef."

"You say that like I should know who she is."

Jason smiled mildly. "Her chocolate cake is one of the top five things I've ever eaten in my life."

"High praise coming from a man who loves to eat."

"It was heaven," Jason said devoutly, closing his eyes. Then he refocused on Nico. "It's just as well you don't know her. She's your type and, if you'd met her, you'd have broken her heart. Then we'd have not just an adversary on our hands but a vengeful woman who was out for your balls."

"It'd have added to the thrill of the hunt."

"You're a seriously disturbed man." He began gathering his contracts and notes.

Unable to help it, Nico asked, "What makes her my type, Jason?"

"Feisty," he said without hesitation. "Face of a Botticelli angel. She's the type of woman you never go for."

He shook his head. "That doesn't make sense. You just said she was my type."

"She is, but you never go for women who have life and substance to them. Instead you go for the obvious and dull. Tall, blond, and icy."

He raised his brows. "Icy?"

Jason shrugged. "I was being kind."

"What makes you think that this Daniela Rossi is better for me?" he asked curiously.

"She's as passionate as you are," Jason said without pause. "She'd stand up to you. You need someone you can't boss around. You tend to pick women who are easily swayed to your way of thinking, let's just say."

"You mean I control them?"

"If you want to be blunt about it."

Nico frowned. "You sound like you know Daniela Rossi well."

"I only met her once, over a slice of her chocolate cake, but it made a lasting impression."

"Apparently." And he didn't like it.

Jason grinned and stood with his briefcase. "You're just jealous you haven't tasted her cake."

Maybe. Maybe he was jealous that someone could enjoy something so small as a piece of cake. He hadn't enjoyed anything in a long time. He was only going through the motions.

But he *would* enjoy tearing down the Harrison Street building. He'd demolish it and erect a marketplace and parking facility, like the Ferry Building. Most importantly, he'd erase the last reminder of where he came from and what he'd lost.

And then…

He shook his head. He'd figure out what then after. First things first. "Get me that building, Jason."

"Of course." Tipping his head, he let himself out.

As soon as he was gone, Nico sat in front of his laptop and opened a browser. Into Google, he typed *Daniela Rossi*.

Chapter Three

Marley walked into the unfinished kitchen of Daniela's West Coast operation and stopped in shock. "Daniela, are you *baking*?"

Her boss grunted, occupied by kneading dough on her special pastry counter.

Marley stared at the sight. Daniela hadn't baked in—well, she couldn't remember the last time, aside from the wedding cake she'd made for the owner of Grounds for Thought, with whom Daniela had bonded.

But there it was, right in front of her eyes: Daniela Rossi with her hands caked in flour and Sinatra crooning softly from the expensive sound system Marley had had installed per Daniela's instructions.

She looked at her boss, trying to figure out what had changed. Daniela wore a pair of yoga pants and a tank top, showing off her toned arms, which were partly credited to Pilates but mostly due to manipulating batter and dough. Her mass of dark curly hair was rolled and pinned on top of her head, a few short strands trailing loose. Her cheeks looked flushed, like she was feverish.

It was the look she got when she was determined.

A determined Daniela never bode well for Marley. It meant her job of wrangling the hot-headed pastry chef was going to be difficult.

But the fact that she was baking had to be a good sign.

Marley slowly backed out of the kitchen, careful not to make another peep. Daniela got extremely focused when she was cooking, and the slightest interruption set off fireworks that rivaled the Fourth of July.

Stepping over construction debris, she let herself out of the showroom, which wasn't completed yet because Daniela was dragging her feet, and went out the front door. She locked it and hurried to the house Daniela's brother had arranged for them to live in.

House was understating things. It was more like a mansion, especially for someone who'd grown up in Manhattan. Four stories on the edge of Laurel

Sweet on You

Heights, it was gaudy as hell, but that was Antonio Rossi's style. Daniela hated the house.

Marley loved it.

Not the whole house, per se, but the basement level that she'd taken over for herself, with Daniela's blessings. She had the entire floor, which included an office, a huge bedroom and sitting room, a bathroom fit for an emperor, a sauna, and a room entirely dedicated to her photography.

She called it her Batcave.

She had a separate entrance that led directly into it, and sometimes when she came back from taking photos at night, she imagined she'd been out fighting crime and was slinking back to her lair.

Her mother, a high-powered editor in New York, would have hated the basement. She'd have tried to light up every corner, complaining about how dreary it was. But then, her mother had never understood her—or even tried to. Marley had always been some foreign creature to her literary mom: a strange girl who loved to be in the shadows and had an obsession for comic books.

When Daniela had declared they were moving to San Francisco, Marley had been torn. The distance

Kate Perry

from her mother would be a blessing. The distance from the man she loved? Torture.

Not that Antonio Rossi knew she loved him. Or even that she existed, for that matter.

She unlocked the door to her Batcave and wound her way through the hallway to her office. Closing the door out of habit, she sat at her desk, blew a kiss to Batman who stared enigmatically from the print she'd hung on the wall, and took her iPhone out of her purse.

Tony answered the phone the way he always did, regardless of caller ID. "Rossi."

Every time Marley heard his voice or saw him walk into a room, she had a moment when she couldn't breathe. Struck completely speechless.

She knew it was ridiculous—she'd been around him in some form or another for seven years—but she couldn't help it. It wasn't that he was gorgeous, which he was. He had that "it" quality movie stars like Brad Pitt and Gerard Butler had, that made you just want to wrap yourself around them and ask them to take you.

Marley was *so* not the kind of woman anyone would take, especially Antonio Rossi. But, goodness, did she want to try.

"Marley?" he asked, concern in his voice. "Are you there?"

"Oh. Yes." She cleared the jittery nerves from her throat. "Daniela's baking."

Silence stretched on the other end of the line. Then he said, "Is she listening to music?"

"Frank Sinatra."

Tony heaved a sigh. "Thank God. Does this mean she's over whatever funk she's been in?"

"I don't know, but it seems promising," she said hopefully. "She hasn't baked anything except one wedding cake in months, and she's only baking bread."

"*Bread?*"

"A lot of it."

After a moment, he said, "Okay, it's a start. It's better than nothing. Listen, Marley, I need you to press her."

She blinked in surprise. "Press her on what?"

"For one thing, finishing up the storefront. Renovation has been going on too long."

"Got it," she said, writing down a note. With Daniela baking again, it shouldn't be too difficult to

Kate Perry

get her to finally tie up all the loose ends with the remodel.

"Additionally, the Food Network wants her to do another show. They see her as the counterpart to Bourdain, traveling around the world, trying desserts. They like that she's like a more feisty Giada de Laurentiis."

That described Daniela a year ago, but her boss hadn't been feisty in months.

Unaware of her thoughts, Tony continued. "It's a fantastic opportunity. She needs to say yes."

"I'm not sure she will," Marley said hesitantly.

"Which is why I need you to press her."

She fell silent, feeling awkward. Daniela wasn't just her boss but her friend, too. Marley knew this was a good opportunity career-wise for Daniela, but was it what she really needed? Because she suspected what the woman really needed was a long stay in a luxury resort, to rest. "I don't know, Tony."

"It's the best thing for her," he said in his smooth voice. "She's been stuck in this rut for too long, and she's immobilized. She just needs to start moving again and she'll be okay. I have her best interests at heart."

She didn't doubt that. Tony and Daniela were enviably close. Marley had been an only child of a single parent, her dad having remarried and started a new family. She'd always wondered whether she and her mother might be closer if there'd been a buffer between them.

Tony was nothing if not an excellent salesman. He didn't disappoint her. He sensed her hesitation and eased in for the kill. "You're the closest one to her right now. You're the one to save her from herself, Marley."

She pictured herself in a cape and big boots. "I don't know."

"I have every confidence in you."

"Really?" She sat up proudly, bolstered by his praise.

"Definitely. You won't let me down."

She nodded. "I won't."

"Good." His tone softened. "You're the best, Marley."

She hung up, still glowing from his praise. Until she started thinking about telling Daniela about the new show.

Daniela was *not* going to be happy.

Marley whirled her chair around and looked balefully at Wonder Woman, who stood guard in a framed poster behind her. "I can't believe I let him schmooze me into agreeing."

Wonder Woman's expression seemed to say *Really?*

She sighed. "I know. Tony's my Kryptonite."

Wonder Woman looked cheerfully unsympathetic.

Marley shook her head and turned around. Next time, she was turning to Aquaman.

Chapter Four

*T*HE BUILDING WAS deserted, a shell of what it used to be regardless of its bright exterior.

Nico stood across the street and studied it, remembering despite himself. When he and his brother had lived there, the building had just been gray and prison-like. The artsy facade had been added a few years ago by a local artist trying to ameliorate the neighborhood.

Nothing would ever make this building happier, in his opinion, but he appreciated that someone tried.

Taking the small bottle of Jim Beam from his pocket, he crossed the street and went up the walkway to sit on the front step. The street lamp flickered and then turned off.

Just as well. The shadows suited him just fine when he came here.

He untwisted the cap and took a grimacing sip.

The stuff was awful, but it'd been his brother's favorite, so that was what he always brought.

He held the bottle up. "*Salud*, Eddie."

He poured the rest of the bottle on the sidewalk, watching it drip down the walkway.

The same way Eddie's blood had.

He closed his eyes and rested his head on his folded hands. It was over twenty years later and he could still see the sight clear as day. Eddie's body riddled with bullets, deposited in front of the building as a message.

A message he'd gotten loud and clear, just not the one the gang had intended. Instead, Nico saw it as Eddie's biggest act as an older brother—a warning not to walk the same path he'd errored down.

Nico had been so close.

Now he owned the world.

And soon he'd own this building. He'd destroy it, finally, the way Eddie had always wanted to do when they were kids.

Nico tipped the last bit of bourbon down the sidewalk and saluted the sky. Getting up, he started down the walkway.

And then he stopped, catching a flash of motion.

He ducked into a shadow, watchful.

A figure crawled out of one of the partially boarded windows of the building.

Nico moved stealthily closer, careful not to give away his presence. Then he frowned. It was a woman—there was no mistaking the curves of her body or the feminine way she moved.

He watched as she walked to a nearby box, pulled out a bundle, and crawled back into the building.

He hurried after her.

The window opening was jagged with broken glass, and his wide shoulders made it more challenging to enter. Using his foot, he broke off the remaining shards of glass and climbed inside.

It was dark, and he saw no sign of her. So he waited.

He didn't have to wait long. Seconds later she rushed toward the window.

Toward him.

She was so focused on her thoughts she didn't see him blocking the window until she was almost on top of him. She uttered a startled gasp, her eyes wide.

She looked small and soft. She had the face of a Renaissance angel, with dark free flowing curls and pure milky skin. Skin he had the urge to touch, and a face he recognized.

Daniella Rossi.

What was she doing here? The last place he'd expect a woman who'd baked for kings, a woman who'd had a popular television cooking show, was climbing through a window of a condemned building.

It intrigued him despite himself.

He searched her eyes, looking for answers. He saw the sorrow of the past and the potential of the future. He saw compassion and passion, like a sea of chocolate he wanted to bathe in—dark and rich, bittersweetly delicious.

His groin tightened.

Those eyes narrowed, and she marched toward him, putting her hands on her hips when she stopped right in front of him. "Don't even think about it," she said, her voice low with warning.

He couldn't help it—he smiled. "I'm already thinking of it."

The man in front of her looked like a thug in sheep's clothing.

Sweet on You

He had all the ingredients for danger: powerful build, dark hair, expensive clothing. The barest hint of sweetness, with his curious gaze. And a dash of spice: the sort of five o'clock shadow that'd rasp the skin of your inner thighs.

He was a recipe for ecstasy.

If he were cake, he'd be Devil's Food—rich and dark. Forbidden. A guilty pleasure you wanted to indulge in secretly.

Daniela licked her lips. Delicious, really.

And *insane*. Here she was: in a dark, condemned building, at dusk, and she was getting it on with him in her head. Tony would have ripped her a new one over her lack of sense.

But she couldn't help it. Something inside her went gooey looking at the stranger.

She shook her head. "I have a death wish."

He tipped his head, watching her carefully. "Why do you say that?"

"You're obviously a threat, but I'm mentally undressing you." She looked him over thoroughly. "Silk."

He blinked once, as though she'd taken him off guard. "Excuse me?" he said in rough voice that was street with a thin veneer of Park Avenue.

"Boxers. You've got rough edges, but I bet you like silk underneath."

He smiled like a wolf. "Want to find out?"

"A woman would have to be stupid not to want to get into your pants." She sighed regretfully. "But I'm busy right now."

"Busy doing what?"

"None of your business," she said tartly, pushing past him and climbing out the window.

She'd expected him to follow her, but he just leaned in the window and watched her.

She lifted a box of small quiches. She'd gone overboard with the food, making way too much for just three people, especially since she doubted they had a way to store any of it. But maybe they'd share it, and she'd wrapped the bread so it'd keep regardless.

Her arms complained as she carried the smaller box back to the window. She glared at the mystery man. "You could help."

"I could, if I knew what I was helping to do." But he took the box from her anyway.

She studied him. "You won't call the police?"

"Why would I?" He sniffed the quiches. "Have

you baked pot into these?"

"Of course not. I'm leaving food for the homeless."

He was silent for a long moment, staring at her. His gaze was probing and direct, but it didn't bother her—Tony looked at people the same way. Besides, she had nothing to be ashamed of.

Finally he said, "You're here in the dark, leaving food for homeless people?"

"It's not completely dark, and don't say it like I'm a fool."

"You *are* a fool, to risk your safety. This is a dangerous neighborhood."

"Please." Pushing her hair over her shoulder, she made a dismissive noise. "I grew up in New York."

He looked like he wanted to argue, but he just said, "Hand me the rest of what's in your box."

She did, quickly, before he changed his mind. When he had it piled in his arms, she told him to go down the hall and leave it where she'd already set the loaves of bread.

He was back quickly, crawling through the window with a grace and ease she wouldn't have expected from a man his size. He brushed off his hands on his expensive jeans and then gestured toward the street. "Let's go."

She sighed, disappointed that he didn't take her hand. "Are you leading me to your lair?" she asked hopefully.

"I'm taking you to a cab." He glanced at her. "You have no sense. You should be scared of me."

"I can't help it. You're all bark. I think you're a marshmallow inside."

He scowled as if the description were distasteful. "No one's ever called me a marshmallow."

"Then no one's ever really looked at you." If they did, they'd notice the sadness under the intelligence and steadiness of his eyes.

Who cooked for him? For some reason, she doubted he'd had a grandmother who taught him about life as she fed him.

It made her sad, too.

She cleared her throat. "What do you like to eat?"

"What?"

"Your favorite food? I bet it's something warm and mushy, like you are on the inside."

He glared at her.

"See?" She grinned. "I was right, wasn't I?"

"You're playing with fire, baby," he said in what was probably his best gangster's voice.

Daniela rolled her eyes. "Please don't say I'm going to get burned. Besides, I know how to handle heat. I'm a chef."

He said nothing, silently contemplating her.

"This is where you say who you are and what you do," she prompted as they walked around the corner, away from the building and onto Mission Street.

"You didn't tell me who you are."

"Daniela." She held her hand out.

He took it and pulled her closer.

Her breath caught as she steadied herself against his chest. Her senses overloaded, with the hot feel of her hand engulfed in his and the hardness of his pecs under her palm. She knew she probably looked like she was caught in headlights.

She had no idea what to do.

It wasn't like she didn't get hit on. A few of her customers, and sometimes their guests, tried to corner her. But she'd never wanted to be cornered quite as badly as she did now.

She'd never felt as wild.

She hadn't felt so much like herself in —

Well, definitely since her birthday, but possibly since her grandmother had died a year ago. Feeling that old cockiness went to her head.

It was such a rush that it made her feel reckless. She closed the distance between them. "Tell me now if you're a serial killer or something, because I'm about to be very foolish, and I want to be warned if I'm making a big mistake."

"I'm in real estate," he said in his dark voice.

Ah—he was here to scope out the building then. Or else he was the one selling it. Either way, now she could do this without worry.

She stood on her tiptoes and kissed him.

It was slow and deliberate, deep and hot. She suddenly knew what melting icing on hot cinnamon rolls felt like.

"Yum." She sighed and nuzzled his scratchy cheek with her nose. "I knew buying this building was a good thing, but I had no idea it'd be this good."

"You aren't buying that building."

"Yes, I am."

He lifted her face. "What the hell would you want that dump for?"

"To turn it into a soup kitchen."

He gazed at her like she was insane. Then he shook his head, took her hand, and flagged a taxi.

"Despite appearances, I'm not really that kind of girl," she said, following him to the curb. "I'm not going home with you, but I wouldn't mind kissing again."

He muttered something that sounded like Spanish under his breath. "I'm putting you in a cab before you cause more trouble."

"You liked my brand of trouble a moment ago," she said, disappointed when a taxi veered and stopped directly in front of them, like it knew better than to defy him.

He opened the door, but before he stuck her inside, he searched her face one more time. Then he shook his head and practically pushed her in.

She told the cab driver to wait a second as she lowered the window. "You should have kissed me again like you wanted to," she said to the stranger.

"Maybe."

He looked so alone, standing there with his hands shoved in his pockets. Her heart wept for him. She wished she could take him home and make him pasta. *A la arrabiata*, hot and spicy, the way she liked it.

She had a feeling he liked it the same way.

"Aren't you going to tell me your name?" she asked.

"What difference would it make?"

"Because I'm going to daydream about your silk boxers, and you wouldn't want me to call you Nigel in my fantasies, would you?"

He grinned despite himself. "Nico."

"Nico." She liked it. Simple. To the point. Strong.

He leaned his forearms on the window, a breath away from her lips.

Would he kiss her? Goose bumps rose all over her body in anticipation.

But he just whispered, "No boxers, baby. I go commando."

He patted the roof of the car, nodding at the driver, who took off.

Daniela sat back and fanned herself. "Nico," she repeated, wondering when she'd see him again. She knew one thing for certain: he'd find her. And she was looking forward to it.

Chapter Five

SITTING ACROSS THE kitchen table, Marley watched her boss poke at the calculator and then scowl at the notepad in front of her. Daniela scribbled a couple things on the notepad and then glared at the calculator again, like it was offending her.

Very strange. Daniela usually avoided complex math like the plague. Anything beyond doubling a pound of flour taxed her.

"Do you need help?" Marley felt compelled to ask, even though it was her morning off.

"No," Daniela barked, jabbing at the old school machine.

"Because I'm happy to help." She lifted her coffee and sipped, leaning forward to get a better look at the notepad. There was a messy jumble of numbers that made no sense, plus a couple hearts doodled on the side.

The heart had a word inside them. She narrowed her eyes, trying to see the small print.

Daniela turned the notepad over with a slap. "You're being nosy."

"It's my job. I'm supposed to help you, even when you don't want it."

Her boss tossed her curly hair over her shoulder. "Sometimes your job sucks."

Tell her about it. Especially when her lovely but temperamental boss refused to discuss business with her.

"Especially when you have to deal with me in one of my moods," Daniela said as if hearing her thoughts. "I'm sorry I'm being witchy."

She shrugged, surprised by the apology. "I could do worse."

"Not since Kim Jong-il died." She flashed a saucy grin. Then she grew serious, leaning forward, her dark gaze searching. "Don't you ever dream of doing something more though?"

Marley blinked at the sudden seriousness, feeling like there was a layer to the question she wasn't getting. "What would I do?"

"I don't know. Be a party planner, or a stripper.

Anything." Daniela waved flamboyantly. "A photographer. You do great pictures."

She sighed, feeling a longing deep in the pit of her stomach. She loved taking photos. Thinking about it made her fingers twitch with the desire to hold her camera.

Only it wasn't practical. Her mother, as a New York editor, had beaten it into her head that most "artists" don't ever make a living at what they do, regardless of their medium. To throw away a great job that took her all over the world and provided her stability would be insane.

But it'd have been *so great*.

She shook her head. "Why? Do you think of doing something other than baking?"

"That'd be crazy, wouldn't it?" Daniela replied thoughtfully.

"Speaking of baking"—Marley cleared her throat—"what happened to all the bread you baked?"

Her boss's face became mulish, as if she expected a fight and wasn't going to give an inch. "I gave it to people."

Damn. Daniela's cinnamon bread was to die for. "All of it?"

"It was my bread, to do with what I wanted."

"Are you going to bake more? For Christmas?"

"No." She shook her head, her hair a frenzy around her face. "Christmas is cancelled this year."

Marley gaped. "But you love Christmas."

"Not this year I don't." She stood up and gathered her things.

"You're leaving? But I still wanted to talk about Tony and the Food—"

"It's your morning off, and I have no desire to talk about my brother." Daniela gave her a flat look. Her arms burdened, she lifted her chin and marched out.

"Okay," Marley said weakly, watching her boss go. "I'll catch up with you later, then."

The lack of response was more an answer than anything.

Marley had one massive headache.

It was the Rossis' fault—both Daniela and Tony's. Tony called her and berated her for not talking to Daniela yet, and Daniela refused to listen to any mention of her brother. It was enough to drive a girl to drink.

And she needed a shot of something strong really badly, and she knew exactly where to get it: Grounds for Thought, the bookstore café across the street from Daniela's shop. For most people, a shot meant alcohol. Marley's poison of choice was coffee, and Grounds for Thought had the best espresso she'd ever tasted.

Taking her wallet, she walked out of her Batcave and down the street. The house was located only four blocks away from the showroom. Anyone else might have thought Tony picked the house for convenience, but really he'd picked it because a commute took away from productive time.

Marley walked briskly back into the heart of Laurel Heights, straight to Grounds for Thought. Her focus was on her shot of espresso, so she didn't notice anyone coming out of the coffeehouse until a man loomed directly in front of her.

A very large man. He had intense dark eyes and a body built like the Hulk, except he wasn't green.

But he *was* angry, based on the way he glared at her. She stood shock-still, caught like a bunny in a lion's path.

"Move," he growled.

With a squeak, she stepped out of his way. She watched him go to the door directly the to left of the café's entrance, leading to the apartments above. He deftly punched a code into the keypad next to the door and went inside when the buzzer sounded.

Rattled, she walked into the café and headed straight to the counter where Valentine Jones and Kristin, the barista, were chatting.

Kristin grinned at her. "Had a run in with the ogre of Laurel Heights, did you?"

"He's more like the Hulk," she murmured, sliding onto a stool.

"I'd like to hook him up with someone," Valentine said.

They both looked at Valentine, who sat primly on a stool.

"I'm a matchmaker, and it'd be good PR. If I can find a mate for him, I should be able to find one for anyone." Then she blinked and focused on Marley. "You."

Marley blinked. "Me?"

"Let me set you up." Valentine made a face. "Not that I'm saying you'd be good PR because you'd be hard to match up with anyone."

Kristin snorted.

They both looked at her.

The barista put her hands in the air. "I'm taken, lock, stock, and barrel. I'll leave you guys to your negotiation. Marley, an espresso?"

"A double." She needed it.

Valentine leaned in toward her after Kristin turned to pull the shot. "Have you seen her guy? *Hot*. Don't tell anyone this, but I couldn't have done better for her myself."

She didn't know Kristin's situation, or the guy she was apparently with, but Marley had a hard time picturing anyone hotter than Tony Rossi.

Kristin returned with the espresso, sliding it across the counter with a wink before going to take another patron's order.

Marley lifted the little cup as Valentine turned to her and said, "So, you."

She shook her head. "No."

"Please?" Valentine gave her puppy dog eyes. Marley figured Valentine couldn't be much younger than her, but she looked young. Maybe it was because she was so thin, but in her 50s homemaker dress and little sweater, she looked like she was playing dress-up.

But then, Marley shouldn't judge. She wore black like she was a backdrop for other people's lives, which was exactly what she was, now that she thought about it. She frowned.

"Just once," the woman was saying. "Go out on just one date and, if you don't like it, I'll never bother you again."

"No."

"Come on. What do you have to lose?"

"Well—" She stopped, stumped. "That's a really good question."

"I'll make it painless," Valentine said eagerly. "I promise. And you only have to go out on one date. Please, Marley. It'll be worth it."

She tried to think of a reason to turn her down, but she couldn't come up with a single one, so for the second time in one day she found herself agreeing to do something she wasn't entirely convinced about. "Only one date."

Valentine squealed and threw her arms around her. "*Thank you*. You won't regret it."

Marley lifted her gaze and met Kristin's amused one. She sighed, already having second thoughts.

Chapter Six

She'd been in some of the most luxurious houses around the world, but Daniela had never been intimidated the way she was sitting in the real estate agent's office.

Not that it was overly fancy. It was tasteful and posh without being excessive. It looked exactly the way she'd expect the office of a successful San Francisco real estate person to look.

Ken Lewis fit his office. Slacks and a dress shirt, no tie, clean cut, moderately nice watch on his wrist. If he were a recipe, he'd have been *tarte tatin*: simple, elegant, and universally accepted.

Daniela crossed her legs and pumped her foot, watching him squint at his computer monitor. Tony had always managed the business stuff for her. He bought the buildings and signed the contracts. She was in charge of fondant and candied violets.

A flutter of nerves made her stomach clench.

She lifted her chin. This was a good idea, and she was smart and capable. She could do this.

"Here it is," Ken said, his fingers clacking clumsily on the keyboard. "The old motel on Harrison, South of Market. The price is certainly low."

"It's a dump."

He looked around his large monitor at her. "But you want it?"

"I want to turn it into a soup kitchen."

"Soup kitchen," he repeated with skepticism.

Nodding, she sat forward on the edge of the chair. "The kitchen is big enough for large-scale production, and the location seems ideal."

"South of Market and the Financial District both have a large population of homeless, and it's central to other areas like the Mission." Ken shrugged. "It seems a little large for what you want, but maybe you could turn some of the rooms into a shelter."

Gasping, she sat up, thinking of the family that was squatting on the property. "A soup kitchen and homeless shelter. Maybe I offer restaurant prep and cooking classes to help people get back on their feet. With restaurant job placement. I certainly have connections. And the housing can be an interim place to live until they can move back into society. It's *brilliant*."

"If you say so yourself?" Ken grinned. "The price is right, and the building really is perfect for what you want. It's a good investment, regardless. Normally, I'd caution a client against this sort of endeavor, but even if you changed your mind, you wouldn't be in danger of losing money. The South of Market area is hot."

"I'm not going to change my mind."

"No, I don't get that impression." He flashed her a quick smile before becoming all business. "I suggest putting in a signed bid slightly lower than the asking price, to give ourselves room to negotiate. I'll draw up the papers so you can sign them before you leave."

"Excellent." She rubbed her hands together.

"I don't foresee the sale taking long, since you're willing to purchase it regardless of its state." He clicked with his mouse a couple times. "We should be able to close in as soon as a couple weeks, all things willing and barring unforeseen snags."

"How often do snags happen?"

"Not too often." He shrugged as his printer

began spitting out pages. "This is all straightforward. It should be simple."

Simple was the best, Nonna always said.

Her grandmother would approve of this, Daniela thought as she signed the bid. Tony wouldn't, but she wasn't going to think about him. This was about her.

Well—her *and* the homeless. It'd be a win-win situation for everyone involved. She was positive about that.

Chapter Seven

Shifting to get comfortable on the stiff Victorian-style chair, Marley looked around the subterranean office and wondered how she got herself talked into this.

"I'm almost ready," Valentine said. She sat in a similar chair, across a glass-top table, looking right at home as she tapped at her phone. "Then we'll find the perfect man for you."

Marley had already found the perfect man—Antonio Rossi. He was everything a man should be: loyal, successful, and strong. Maybe Valentine could set her up with him.

As if he'd agree to be set up. He was as difficult as his sister.

She thought of Daniela and her stomach burned, like stress was eating a hole in it. Of course, it was possible she'd just had too much coffee today.

No—Marley shook her head—it was the stress in dealing with her boss that was disrupting her system. Daniela had sequestered herself away in her room for days, obviously plotting something big. When she did emerge from behind her locked door, she had a dreamy-but-determined look that put fear in Marley's heart.

That look never boded well for anyone. She'd spent the morning making a list of what Daniela could be plotting, and none of it had been good. It'd finally driven her out of the house and straight to Valentine's, for respite.

She sighed and looked longingly at the door. The office was small—one lunge and she'd be outside. It was partly underground, but the long window along the sidewalk let in a lot of light. Of course, the brightness of the space may have been due to the gilded furnishings and mirrored surfaces all over the room.

It made for an uncomfortable setting. Marley wasn't a creature of the light. She much preferred the shadows. "Valentine, maybe this wasn't a good idea."

"Honestly, Marley? You're doing me a huge favor. Really." Valentine leaned forward. "I haven't matched anyone since I opened up my shop. If

I could just have one success story, then I'd attract more business."

"I know, but—"

"It's Christmas time and you just moved to the city," Valentine continued. "Aren't you lonely? This is the best time of year to start a meaningful relationship."

"Yes, but—"

"I won't charge you for this," Valentine interjected.

Marley couldn't help smiling. "You're determined."

"Yes."

She'd already met the man she wanted, but the desperate look in the other woman's eyes made her sigh. "I only have to go on one date?"

"Yes."

She sighed again. "Okay."

"You aren't going to bolt?"

"No."

The relief on Valentine's face was almost comical. *Thank you.* Let's get started so we can get you out of here. I just need to pull up a fresh questionnaire for you."

Marley watched her, fascinated. "You do this on your phone?"

"I don't like having a big monitor between me and my clients, so I created an app to use."

"Really?" she said, impressed.

"It was no big deal. It creates more intimacy this way." The matchmaker flushed, her pale red-head's skin looking painfully red. She lowered her head to study the screen. "So what's your sign?"

"Seriously?" Marley frowned. "That's how you're going to pick Mr. Perfect for me?"

"Once you see how genius I am at this you won't mock my methods. But, fine, next question." She typed something into her computer and then asked, "How many children do you want?"

"I haven't thought about it."

"What? How can that be true?

Because she had no idea what Tony thought about it, and she was open to the possibilities. "I was an only child. I don't know how I feel about children."

Shaking her head, Valentine tapped at her phone, a frenzy of thumbs. The mirror behind her reflected the back of her head, adding a halo around her red hair, making her look like a fiercely focused Madonna who liked her electronic device.

Without thought Marley pulled out her iPhone,

opened her camera function, and began snapping pictures. It wasn't as good as her Nikon digital SLR. But with some manipulation her phone still took great pictures, and she had it with her all the time.

Valentine glanced up. "Photo op time?"

"Sorry." She took another picture. "I can't help myself."

"I don't mind. I can even strike a pose for you if you want." She grinned crookedly.

Marley couldn't resist taking one more. That was the one—the light was perfect and Valentine's personality would shine through the flat image. She tucked the phone away. "I'll give you a copy of that last one."

"So you like to take pictures?" Valentine asked with the interest of a scientist.

"It's just a hobby I picked up a long time ago."

"The look on your face as you were taking pictures of me suggested otherwise."

"What look on my face?" she asked cautiously.

"Total concentration. You were utterly engrossed. You obviously feel passionate about it."

She shrugged. "It's just what I do."

"What else are you passionate about?"

"Comics," she said without thinking. She blushed at the startled way Valentine stared at her. "I know. It's a geeky thing, but I can't help it. The characters are so great."

"Comics." The matchmaker's lips pursed. "Okay, I think I have enough to go on to find you the perfect man."

A niggle of nervousness jangled her stomach. She pressed a hand to her middle. "I don't know about this. I'm not good at dating."

"You just need practice, and you're in luck. I give lessons. All part of the service." She stood up. "I'm going to go through my database of possible matches. I'll have the man I choose call you."

Marley stood up slowly, having second, third, and fourth thoughts about what she'd agreed to. "Just one date. That's all I promised."

"That's all I'll need," Valentine said with her crooked grin. She turned and held the door open for Marley. "Talk to you soon. Real soon."

Marley shook her head and mumbled to herself. "Why did that sound like a threat?"

She hurried home, trying to put her meeting with

Valentine out of her mind. She needed to focus on Daniela and convincing her to take the Food Network gig.

But all afternoon, she couldn't realign her thoughts. She kept thinking about the impending date and feeling guilty about it.

It felt like she was cheating on Tony.

Which was absolutely ridiculous. She knew it. It wasn't like Antonio Rossi even realized she was alive—yet—but she still felt like she was doing something wrong. Even the Justice League seemed to be looking at her in reproach.

Finally, she decided to take a break from work. Twenty minutes in the sauna and she'd be clear-headed again.

In her bedroom, she undressed. Grabbing a towel from the bathroom, she wrapped it around herself and toed on her slippers before padding down the hallway.

Her phone rang as she let herself into her private spa, as she liked to call it. She answered it, even though she didn't recognize the number.

"Is this Marley?" a man's voice asked.

Turning on the sauna to let it heat, she got ready

to brush off the marketing call. "Who is this please?"

"My name is Brian Benedict. Valentine gave me your number and instructed me to call."

Sigh. She hadn't expected someone to call to soon. But she promised one date—she could do this. "Fine. When do you want to do this?"

There was a silence on the line. "You don't sound enthusiastic about meeting me. What if I'm the man of your dreams?"

She snorted as she tested the room. Not warm enough yet. "I think we both know that the chances of the two of us being the right one for each other is really small."

"I don't know any such thing," he replied, sounding as though he were suddenly paying attention.

"Great, now I've intrigued you." She kicked off her slippers. "This isn't a challenge."

He chuckled. "Marley, you definitely sound like a challenge."

"Look, why don't we set up the date? Then I can prove to you aren't interested in me, and we can both move on."

"What are you doing right now?"

"Excuse me?"

"Now. Meet me."

"But it's only"—she held her phone away for a second to look at the time—"four in the afternoon. Don't you have a job?"

"I work from home. Valentine said you did too. You're in Laurel Heights, right? I'll come over."

She looked down at the boob her falling towel exposed. "You can't come over."

"Why not?"

"I'm indecent."

"That's okay, Marley. I won't judge."

"No. I mean I'm not dressed. I was about to step into the sauna."

"Then warm up and meet me. There's that coffee shop Valentine likes, close to her office. What's it called?"

"Grounds for Thought."

"I'll meet you there in half an hour." He paused. "Don't stand me up, Marley."

In his pause, she heard a smile. But she shook her head vehemently. "Brian, I—"

But he already hung up.

She looked at her caller ID, to call him back, but it was a restricted number. She shook her fist at the phone, grumbling, and turned the sauna back off. Apparently she had a date to get dressed for.

She stomped into Grounds for Thought and glared at all the patrons.

One man sitting alone in the corner grinned at her. He winked from behind geeky glasses that were oddly attractive. His hair was messy, like he was a couple weeks overdue for a haircut. He wore jeans and a plaid long-sleeve shirt.

And red Converse shoes.

Valentine had set her up with an older Peter Parker.

Marley shook her head, trying to clear the sudden daydreams of flying through the sky with him on his web. This guy was *not* Spiderman or anything like him. He was some random man who needed to use a dating service—that was it.

Steeling herself, she stormed toward him. "Brian Benedict?"

"I can tell by your charming demeanor you're Marley." He stood up and took her hand, which she hadn't offered. "The pleasure is obviously only mine."

She would *not* be charmed by him. She withdrew her hand and plopped inelegantly onto the chair across from him. "Let's get this over with."

He grinned. "Tell me how you really feel about meeting up with me, Marley."

She stifled the beginning of a smile. It'd be really inconvenient to like him. Besides, he seemed like a nice guy, and she didn't want to lead him on. "Look, I need to be honest with you. I'm doing this as a favor to Valentine. I'm not looking for anyone. I've already met the man for me."

"Where is he?"

She blinked, surprised by the question. "Excuse me?"

"Where is he?" Brian craned his neck, looking over and around her. "Is he going to storm in here and kick my ass?"

"Of course not. He's in New York."

"Then why are you here?"

She shook her head. "I don't understand what you're after."

"And I don't get how you could be dating someone on the other side of the country. It'd make kissing really difficult."

"Tony's never kissed me." Her eyes widened as she realized what she admitted. "I mean, he and I aren't dating, per se."

"Ah."

That one utterance was loaded with meaning. She narrowed her eyes at him. "What does that mean?"

"It means I'm going to buy you coffee." He stood up. "And maybe a treat?"

"No treat."

Grinning, he touched her shoulder as he walked by.

It should have been an inconsequential, glancing touch that meant nothing, but for some reason she got a jolt from it. She was still pondering the residual shockwaves when he returned.

He set a double espresso in front of her. "The barista said you'd like this."

She stared at the little cup, oddly off balance.

"And I brought a cookie to share." He slid the plate toward her. "I hope you like chocolate chip. I couldn't resist."

Because she didn't know what to say, she lifted her cup and took a sip. She closed her eyes, it was so delicious going down.

When she reopened her eyes, Brian was staring at her. She glared at him to cover up her discomfort. "What?"

He shook his head. "Tell me about your true love."

"My who?"

"The guy in New York who you're saving yourself for. What's he like?"

"Why?"

"I want to know what I'm up against."

She shook her head. "You're not up against anything. In any case, I'm not dating him yet."

"Is he married?"

"No."

"He has a girlfriend?"

"No." Not that she knew of. At least, no one serious.

Brian nodded, sitting back, legs crossed so his red Converse were in her view. "Then he's either a player or a hermit."

"He's not a hermit." Antonio Rossi *did* like women—plural—but she was too loyal to call him a player. "He just hasn't found the right woman yet."

"Hmm."

"What does that mean?"

"It means I question his sanity if he can't recognize a great woman, especially right in front of him."

"Do you mean me?"

He rolled his eyes. "Who else would I mean?"

"Why would you say that?" She wrinkled her nose. "I've been awful to you since I walked in here, and you're complimenting me like you mean it."

"I do mean it." He lifted his coffee cup to his mouth, his gaze steady on hers. "I've been in your presence for ten minutes, and I can tell, while not the most charming lady, you're loyal, passionate, and caring."

"How can you tell that?"

"Loyal." He held up a finger. "You're not dating this guy, who, incidentally, doesn't deserve you, and you feel compelled not to cheat on him."

"I—"

"Two," Brian said loudly, over her, holding up a second finger. "You drank your espresso like it was nectar from the gods. For a second I thought you were going to orgasm right here. Not that I'd have had a problem with that."

She frowned to keep from smiling. "And three?"

"Caring." He held out half the cookie to her. "You cared enough about me, a stranger, to warn me away from you. You didn't want to break my heart. That's sweet."

"I'm not sweet."

"No, Marley, you really aren't. You're more like dark chocolate, bittersweet and murky." He leaned forward, his eyes glinting with mischief. "But I love chocolate."

She would *not* like him, she told herself. "Back off, Brian Benedict."

"Not a chance. Not even your clothing can scare me away."

The determination in his eyes sent shivers up her spine—shivers of anticipation, she realized with surprise.

Then she registered what he said. "What's wrong with my clothing?" she asked indignantly. Her outfit was from Ann Taylor.

"You're dressed like an undertaker."

"I am not. Black is chic."

"If you're the Black Widow."

"Batman wore black," she pointed out. "And Batman is cool."

"Batman lurks in the shadows."

"You say that as if it's a bad thing."

"Maybe it's time to step out of the shadows, Marley." Brian Benedict stood, settling his glasses higher on his nose. "Maybe it's your time to shine."

Before she could reply, he touched her shoulder again, smiled, and left the café.

She sat, dumbfounded, staring after him. She put her hand on the spot he'd touch, feeling the pressure through the layers of her clothes. Feeling like the foundation of her world had somehow just shifted.

Chapter Eight

*N*OSTALGIA MADE HER set aside the plans for her soup kitchen and pull out her grandmother's Christmas recipes.

Daniela took the box to her bedroom and sat in the window seat. She wanted to have the idea for her foundation fully formed by the time she bought the Harrison building, but in brainstorming cooking classes to offer and considering recipes, she started thinking about Nonna. If Nonna were still alive, she'd discuss all this with her.

Setting aside the lid for the recipe box, Daniela slowly sifted through the pieces of paper and note cards. The recipes greeted her like old friends.

Nonna's sugar cookie recipe, which guaranteed to cheer up an unhappy child.

Fig tart, voluptuous and ripe.

Torta di mele, with apples, to warm you up on a

cold Fall afternoon.

She arranged them in piles. Each year when she'd return home, she and Nonna would examine all the recipes and decide which ones to make.

Last year, Nonna died before Christmas, and Daniela hadn't had the heart to make anything. She'd started out this season feeling the same way. With Tony on her shit list and her parents traveling the world, who would she bake for?

Christmas baking was about love and intimacy. She was close to Marley, but in the end she knew Marley's loyalty lay with Tony. The crush Marley had on him was painful to behold. Daniela wanted to tell the young woman she could do much better than her self-centered brother.

"The jerk," she murmured, setting aside a recipe for *bocconotti*, one of Tony's favorites. Not that she was going to make it, because he didn't deserve it.

She *missed* him.

She blinked away the sudden tears and flipped carefully through more recipes, trying not to think about the holidays and being alone.

Mostaciolli.

She held up the scrap of paper, remembering

Nonna handing it to her after Poppi, her grandfather, had passed away. Nonna had told her to keep it safe, that it was a recipe to make for a beloved, to inspire passion. Chocolate, cinnamon, cloves, rum... "The ingredients of love, Dani," Nonna had said.

Dark and spicy.

It made her think of Nico.

He hadn't found her yet.

He would. She set aside the recipe. And when he did, she'd make these cookies for him.

Her phone rang, and just like every time this week, her heart leapt when she saw a number she didn't recognize. She answered quickly.

But it was just Ken Lewis, her real estate guy. "We've hit a snag," he said without preamble.

She sat up at his grim tone. "What snag?"

"There's another offer in for the building."

"Can't we just make a higher counter offer?"

"Normally I'd say yes, but we're dealing with Cruz Enterprises."

She didn't know that company, but Ken said it like the name had significance. "What does that mean?"

"Nico Cruz runs Cruz Enterprises," he said, as if that explained everything.

Nico Cruz. Her Nico? How many Nicos could there be in San Francisco?

Well, probably a lot. But how many would bid on the same building she wanted, after she told him she was going to buy it?

She smiled slowly, excitement filling her chest. He'd done it — he'd found her. She laughed. "How clever of him."

"You know him?" Ken asked, sounding intrigued.

"No." She didn't know anything about him except that he went commando and kissed like a fallen angel. She laughed again, shaking her head.

"Are you okay?" the real estate agent asked with concern.

"I will be." Once she'd kissed him again. "Do you have an address for him?"

"His offices are downtown. Hold on." Ken recited an address in the heart of the financial district. "But if you're planning on talking to him, it won't do any good. You might as well save your time to look for a new building to purchase."

"Why do you say that?" she asked.

"Do you know Donald Trump?"

"Of course."

"Cruz is also in real estate development, but he makes Trump look like a pansy." Ken paused, as if letting her absorb his words. "If Nico Cruz wants this property, you don't stand a chance of getting it. He's relentless and has pockets so deep that he could fit a semi in them."

Smiling, she tore off the address and stuck it in her pocket. "You need to work on your analogies."

"Maybe, but that doesn't change the fact that he has more money than you and I combined."

Only she knew that Nico didn't really want the building—Nico wanted to see her again. The building was just a means. But she couldn't tell Ken that. He'd think she was insane.

She probably was, regardless.

"Ken, make a counteroffer, but only for a little above the price he named." She opened her gigantic walk-in closet and picked a dress. It was tomato red, and the hem flirted playfully with her thighs when she walked. Nico wouldn't be able to resist it.

"Daniela, if Cruz wants the building, he's going to get it. Cruz Enterprises will make an offer the owner won't want to refuse. You don't have the kind of money to go up against that."

But Nico didn't want the building. This was just a ploy to get to her—she'd bet her award-winning chocolate cake recipe on it. "Just do it, Ken."

"Don't say I didn't warn you." He sighed. "But since we're doing this, I'd like to suggest putting in a deposit with the counteroffer. It'll show that you're serious about the purchase. I think five-percent of the offer should suffice."

"Okay, if it'll make you happy." She took the clip out of her hair and shook her head. "But I don't plan on losing, Ken."

"You know, if anyone could win against Nico Cruz, it'd be you." He chuckled. "I can't wait to see what happens."

"Brace yourself for fireworks." If only he knew how true that was. She hung up the phone and ran into the bathroom. A shower, some sprucing, and she was out the door and headed downtown.

The guards at the front desk in the lobby stopped talking when she entered.

She strode right up to them, her heels clacking with purpose. "I'm here to see Nico Cruz."

The one seated at the desk tapped something on his keyboard. "Is Mr. Cruz expecting you?"

"In a manner of speaking," she answered with a smile. "I can guarantee he'll want to see me."

The guards exchanged looks she read as *yeah, right*. But the one manning the desk picked up the phone. "What's your name?"

"Daniela Rossi."

The guard lowered his voice as he spoke into the receiver. He paused, shrugged, and then nodded before he hung up. "You can go up," he said as though he were surprised.

She tossed her hair over her shoulder as she walked to the elevator. The other guard followed her and swiped her into it. "It'll take you up to the top."

"Thank you," she said as the door closed.

It was so smooth a ride that she didn't realize how far up she'd gone, or how quickly, until she stepped out and saw the view of the city from the windows around the reception area.

A beautiful blond receptionist, sitting behind a long elegant counter, smiled politely as she stood. "Ms. Rossi? Nico's waiting for you in his office. This way."

Daniela followed the cliché down the hallway and to the right, all the way to the end. The receptionist knocked lightly and then, at the muffled sound, opened it and gestured Daniela inside.

She lifted her head and strode in.

He sat behind his desk. He was groomed perfectly, wearing an expensive shirt with the cuffs rolled up, a Patek Philippe watch flashing at his wrist, and still he looked like he could have easily slipped into the underworld. Everything about him screamed that he wasn't safe.

But safety was overrated. She was willing to risk it. Based on their one kiss, the rewards seemed so worth it. "You found me," she said.

He stood up, his gaze lingering on her legs. "You knew I would."

She dropped her purse on the nearest chair and sauntered right up to him. "The question is, what are we going to do about it now?"

"I have an idea or two." He ran a fingertip along the ridge of her collarbone.

She shivered, feeling the slight touch all over her body. "I hope they include you, me, and a bed."

"They do." He lifted her chin. "Eventually."

She went molten the second his lips touched hers. This was what she'd needed all week. She wound her arms around his neck and gave herself up to it.

To him.

She'd been worried that she'd imagined how outstanding their first kiss had been, but she shouldn't have worried. It was exactly how she remembered it, rich and delicious.

He kissed his way down, giving her goose bumps when he paused at crook of her neck and inhaled.

She sighed in delight, closing her eyes to savor the feeling. "It was clever of you to put in the fake bid on the building to meet me."

"It wasn't fake." He nipped her skin with his teeth.

"I—" Her shiver of pleasure ended abruptly as his words registered. She pulled back enough to look him in the eye. "What?"

"I wanted to see you again, but I want to buy the building, too."

She pulled out of his arms. "Well, you can't have both."

He pulled her close again and showed her differently.

Daniela tried to resist but he was like her mojito cake: intoxicating and too tempting to deny.

She pushed at his chest to give herself enough space to breathe. Even though her lips throbbed with the memory of his kiss, she glared at him. "You're a bastard."

He smiled self-deprecatingly. "By birth and by nature."

He spoke without sentiment, but she still heard a touch of sadness there, and her heart bled for him.

But she steeled herself, refusing to be played for a sucker. "You aren't going to soften me up with sob stories of your poor youth. You're a powerful man now, with everything the world has to offer, and I won't feel sorry for you. You overcame your past."

He studied her intently but said nothing.

So she got right in his face, trying to ignore the yummy scent of him, like bay rum and spices. "I want that building so that I can give other people a chance to overcome their pasts. Surely you can understand that."

He shook his head. "There are other buildings where you can do that."

"But this one is perfect." She thought of the time and expense of installing an industrial-grade kitchen into another space and shuddered. "Why do you need *that* building? Apparently you own half of the world. Can't you find some other spot to exploit?"

"No," he said simply, staring at her with a guarded gaze.

She stared right back, nose to nose. "I'm not going to back down, you know."

He smiled. "I'd be disappointed if you did."

"You're going to be especially disappointed when I take the building right out from under you," she said smugly.

He crowded her. "It's not wise to taunt the lion in his den."

Hands on her hips, she held her ground. "What are you going to do? Eat me up?"

"Exactly." He lowered his head and kissed her again.

Even now that she knew better, it transported her to that place where nothing else existed. As if to make a point, he held her there with just the pull of his lips, no hands, nothing to stop her from stepping away.

As if she'd be crazy enough to step away from this.

She moaned softly and leaned against him, bracing herself on his muscular biceps. She felt the full length of his body against her own curves—aware of the part of his body that seemed particularly happy she was there.

She mewled, liking that she'd turned him on so much so quickly, with nothing but a kiss. Imagine if she really tried.

She broke away with a sigh. "You're really good at that."

"I'm good at more than that."

"I bet." She grinned saucily at him and then headed to the door. Before she stepped out, she looked over her shoulder. "I'm determined to buy that building."

He put his hands in his pockets. "I know you are."

"Nothing's going to change my mind."

"Mine either." His eyes glittered. "I love a challenge."

So did she. She grinned. "Game on, then."

Chapter Nine

Marley sat in her office, cell phone in hand, wondering where Daniela was. She wasn't answering her phone, and she was nowhere in the house. Although if she'd been hiding in a cranny somewhere, it'd have taken Marley days to find her, the house was so big.

Something was obviously up with her boss. She wished she knew what it was.

Her phone buzzed with a text. She glanced down, her heart leaping when she saw it was from Tony. *Any progress with D?*

She turned the screen off.

Then her phone rang.

She jumped, blinking at it. She wouldn't be surprised if Tony had sensed she was ignoring him. He wouldn't stand for that sort of treatment.

But when she looked at the caller ID it wasn't

Tony. It was Brian Benedict.

Should she answer it?

Her head said no, but a small corner of her heart goaded her into picking up the phone. "What do you want?" she asked without preamble.

"Another date," he said, apparently unfazed by her rudeness. "What are you doing right now?"

"I'm working." She looked at the time. "That's usually what people do at eleven-thirty in the morning."

"No, they're usually checking Facebook and thinking about what they'd like to eat for lunch. So what's it going to be?"

"What?"

"Lunch."

She shook her head. "What are you saying?"

"Have lunch with me."

"No," she said automatically.

"Why not? I already know you eat, and you can't tell me you're working."

"Why can't I?"

"Because you're talking to me. Unless you have some sort of incredible concentration splitting abilities, you wouldn't be able to divide your attention between the two. Of course," he continued, "I have no idea what sort of job you have. For all I know, you're carving out hearts while you talk on your Bluetooth headset."

She couldn't help smiling at that image. "Maybe."

"I was hoping to ask you all those things at lunch today, because our introductory meeting didn't cover the usual essentials. My curiosity is burning so bright that I'm even willing to come to Laurel Heights to pick you up."

"No," she said again, less forcefully this time.

He chuckled. "I'm wearing you down."

"Look, Brian Benedict, your persistence is flattering, but you're wasting your time. I already told you I've met the right man for me."

He was silent on the other end of the line. For a second, she thought she'd won the argument and he was going to go away, which made her oddly disappointed. But then he said, "Don't you need another friend?"

"Friend?"

"You say that like it's a foreign concept. Didn't you just move here? You must need friends."

She had so few friends in New York that it hadn't

occurred to her. She'd always been a loner, preferring comic book heroes to real people. They were flawed, but in the end they came through. You couldn't say that about real people.

"Come on, Marley. Just one lunch. If you don't have fun, you don't have to see me ever again. Your obligation to Valentine is already met."

"I—"

"Excellent!" he exclaimed. "Meet me at the corner of Sacramento and Laurel in fifteen."

Before she could say no, he hung up.

"Damn it." She turned her phone off and faced Wonder Woman. "He's determined, I'll give him that."

She played it cool, answering a couple emails and adding a few things to her calendar, before she got up and went to her bathroom, smoothing back her hair and touching up her lipstick.

Even with the little bit of color on her lips, she wondered if she looked too somber, dressed in all black. Brian had thought so last time.

Did she care?

Just a splash of color, she decided. She went in her closet and pulled out a bright scarf Daniela had given her ages ago. Wrapping it around her neck, she went to meet him.

He wasn't there when she arrived. She checked the time. She was three minutes late—he should have been here. The only person nearby was a guy on a sleek black motorcycle, wearing a leather jacket.

And red Converse shoes.

She blinked. Brian Benedict?

He took of his helmet, hanging it on the handlebars, and grinned at her. "Hey Marley."

She blinked again, stunned by how studly he looked on the motorcycle. Kind of like a young Wolverine with glasses. "This is yours?"

"It was a splurge." He patted it with his gloved hand. "But so worth it."

"That's awfully"—*hot*—"dangerous."

"Not if you know what you're doing." He opened a compartment on the back and took out gloves and another helmet. "Put these on."

She took a step back. "I can't get on there."

"Why not?"

"Because I—" She didn't know why, actually. Because he'd surprised her with this facet of himself, and she felt off-kilter.

"I'll drive safely. I promise." He got off and walked toward her.

Except it looked like stalking, and she took another step back. "Brian—"

"Nice scarf." He took the edges and tugged her closer. "It matches your eyes."

"It's lime green."

"It's bright, and so are your eyes when they aren't so defensive." He smiled.

She swallowed, taken aback by his nearness. It was intriguing.

"Your eyes say you want to do it," he said softly.

Kiss him? She shook her head, knowing she was in denial.

"Come on. I can tell you want a ride."

"Oh. The bike." She frowned, off-balance.

"I'll have you to lunch and back safely. I promise."

He was so close she noticed the gray-blue of his eyes behind his glasses. They looked calm and inviting, and they encouraged her to nod and say, "Okay."

"Good." He secured the scarf around her neck and then gently slid the helmet on her head, fastening the strap under her chin with care. "This is going to mess up your hair. Sorry."

"I'm not out to impress anyone."

"I like that." Grinning, he handed her the gloves and got back on. After he put his helmet on, he lifted the kickstand and motioned her on.

It was surprisingly tricky getting her leg over the seat. It took her two tries, but at least he didn't laugh at her.

He took her hands and wrapped them around him—close. She rolled her eyes, knowing this was gratuitous, but deciding not to argue for safety's sake.

He gave her a questioning thumbs up.

She nodded, and they were off.

She thought she'd be scared but she was excited from the moment he pulled out from the curb. She felt the power of the machine under her, reverberating through her, and she loved it. She leaned closer to him, bumping her helmet against his.

They arrived wherever they were going way too quickly. She slid off, already looking forward to the ride back.

Brian parked the bike and took his helmet off. "How did you like that?"

"It was *amazing*." She handed him her headgear and watched him secure them to his bike. "But that doesn't mean I'm going to change my mind about dating you."

"I don't even want to date you anymore, Marley."

Marley eyed him suspiciously. "You don't?"

"You're too high maintenance. We're just going to be friends." Brian raked a hand through his hair and gestured toward the restaurant a couple doors down. "Swan Oyster Depot. They have great seafood here."

There? She looked disbelieving at the restaurant. It was a nondescript entrance on a dingy street, next to a liquor store, with a short line of people waiting to get in. Across the street was sex-toy shop. "You take me to all the nice places."

He grinned at her as they got into line. Then he frowned at her and reached for her head.

"What are you doing?" she exclaimed, batting his hands away.

"Your hair is messy from the helmet." He pulled out the clip that held her hair in its bun and fluffed her hair around her shoulders. "That's better," he said, handing her the clip.

"No it's not." She wound her hair back and reset it in place.

Brian shook his head. "It was pretty down."

"But messy."

"Sometimes messy is what you need."

"I was never allowed to be messy." She winced. Why did she say that? She hadn't meant to—it'd come from nowhere, even if it were true.

Of course Brian glommed on to it. "Not even when you were a kid?"

"My mom preferred things to be tidy."

"And your dad?" he asked as they moved up to stand in the doorway.

"My dad left before I was born," she admitted reluctantly.

She waited for Brian to start extrapolating her neuroses and accredit them to not having a father figure, but all he said was, "What a loser."

She stared at him in shock. Then she nodded. "He really was."

A guy in a white apron gestured to them. "Two of you? Take the spot down at the end."

They walked inside. The only seating was at a long counter. Brian led the way and sat on a stool. She perched primly next to him, hitching her stuff on the hook under the counter.

"They pretty much only serve fresh seafood. I

recommend the salad, unless you like oysters."

The guy in the soiled apron came by, smiling in welcome. They ordered, a half salad for her, a full for him, and two Cokes.

While they waited for their food to arrive, Brian turned to face her. "Since we're going to be friends, you need to fill me in on all the pertinent information. Like what you do for a living."

"I'm the assistant to a world-renowned pastry chef."

"Really?" He perked up. "Do you get leftovers?"

"There usually aren't any." She smiled at his disappointed expression. "At Christmastime she usually bakes at home, but I don't think she will again this year."

"Why is that?"

"Her grandmother died last year. They used to do Christmas baking together. I think Daniela still misses her."

"If anything changes and you have too many cookies on your hands, let me know. I'm very willing to save you from sugar overdose."

She imagined him in a mask, swiping extra cookies out of her way, keeping her hips safe from extra pounds. It wasn't hard to picture, and that made her nervous. So she veered the conversation. "If I were going to be a superhero, I'd be Catwoman."

"I'd have figured you for Wonder Woman. Batman was always my favorite comic book series. Bruce Wayne had an edge, and cool toys."

She sighed. "In a perfect world, he'd really exist."

Brian leaned forward. "If I dressed up as Batman, would you go out with me?"

"I thought you said you didn't want to date me."

"Hypothetically speaking."

"Then, hypothetically speaking, it couldn't hurt." She pictured him in a black latex suit. He'd look sizzling actually. She picked up her Coke and sipped a little, trying to cool herself off.

"Good to know." He smiled and said thanks to the guy who brought them their salads. "I'm an accountant."

She paused with her fork halfway to her mouth. "Brian Benedict, the bookkeeper?"

He shrugged, seemingly not bothered. "Alliteration always worked for Stan Lee. I like numbers, and being an accountant is more creative than you'd imagine."

"I guess," she murmured.

"My clients appreciate me, I make a good living, and since I work for myself I have a fair amount of freedom. Except during tax season." He grinned. "Still, it's not as cool as working with a pastry chef."

"That's not as cool as it sounds. You think *I'm* high maintenance. You should see Daniela." Realizing what she said, she quickly amended her statement. "Not that she isn't great. She's very caring, but she's temperamental."

"Like?" He took a bite of salad and waited for her to explain.

"Like if you interrupt her when she's working, she flips out. And she's picky about the jobs she takes."

"That's a good thing though. I'm picky about the clients I take on."

"But you wouldn't turn down clients who forward your career."

"I might, if they were a pain in the ass." He pointed at her with his fork. "But Daniela's being stubborn about something that's bothering you."

"Is it that obvious?"

"You're like an open comic book." He smiled. "Tell me about it."

"The Food Network wants her to do another show but she won't even let me tell her the terms." Marley picked at her salad, thinking about it. "She's got something else going on, and it's distracting her from her business, and I can't figure it out."

"Maybe she met a guy."

"Daniela?" Marley frowned, trying to picture that. There were always men who wanted her boss. And why not? She was petite and striking and passionate. But Daniela was always disinterested in getting involved beyond a fling every now and then. "I don't know. Whatever it is, I need to figure it out soon."

"You will," Brian said confidently.

"Why are you single?" She studied him, trying to puzzle him out. "You're nice, employed, and decent looking."

"Gee. Thanks." He rolled his eyes.

"It just seems like you'd be able to find dates without employing a matchmaking service."

He blushed. "Actually, Valentine and I dated very briefly. We weren't good together, but we stayed great friends. She asked me to do this favor for her."

Marley stared at him and then started to laugh.

"What's so funny?"

She shook her head, trying to catch her breath. "So all those questions she asked me about how many children I wanted were in vain?"

"Actually, Valentine is good at matching people up. She comes by it naturally. Her mother and grandmother were both matchmakers. She's just awful at pairing herself with anyone." He shook his head. "It defies logic. Lots of guys go out with her too. They become totally devoted to her and are at her beck and call, but none of them fall for her. It's strange and ironic."

"Do you think there's one right person for everyone? Or do you think there are people who are good enough?"

"There's not one right person." He faced her, meeting her eyes seriously. "I think we find someone who clicks and then have to work to make it right. When you stop working, it falls apart. Most people are lazy and just want it to be perfect, but a relationship takes effort."

"So how *is* it you aren't with someone?"

"Maybe I'm waiting for Catwoman, just like you're waiting for Batman."

It wasn't Batman she was waiting for—it was Antonio Rossi. Batman was flawed but, as far as she could tell, Tony was perfect. It made winning him more difficult.

But not impossible, especially if she got Daniela to agree to the Food Network deal.

"Is waiting for Catwoman worth it?" she asked Brian on a whim.

"Hell yes, but then I seem to have a thing for surly women." He dropped some bills on the counter and then stood. "Ready?"

She nodded, surprisingly reluctant to have lunch end. She shoved away the feeling, knowing it was residual from the bike ride.

Which was just as excellent on the way home.

Chapter Ten

"Look at this." Lola held up a package. "It talks, it flashes, *and* it shoots."

Daniela looked up from the doll she held in her hands. "A talking and flashing toy gun?"

"Can you believe it?" She put it back on the shelf. "When I was a kid, the fanciest toy on the market was Barbie's Corvette."

"I had Barbie's Corvette, but my brother used to steal it and have his action figures cruise in it."

"I played with blocks. Do they even have blocks anymore?"

"If they do, they sparkle and make phone calls now." Winking at her friend, Daniela dropped the doll in her cart and rolled down the aisle.

Lola strolled alongside her, hands in the pockets of her hoodie. "You never told me what we're doing here."

"We're buying things." Shopping with a friend was always more fun, and doing it before they headed to Eve's house for girls' night seemed like as good a time as any.

"I see that. But who are we buying for? Your nieces and nephews?"

"I don't have any." She tried to picture Tony with children. At one time, he'd have made a great father, but now she could only see him telling his kids not to get their sticky fingers on his five thousand dollar suit. Of course, she may have been a little biased.

The jerk.

"So…?" Lola waited expectantly.

"It's just Christmas presents for a couple kids I know." A slight exaggeration, because she didn't really *know* Jimmy and his sister, but whatever. She was responsible for them. "Does this place have clothing?"

"I think so, but it's all last season," Lola joked, pointing toward the other side of the children's store.

Although calling it a "store" was grossly understated. It was more of a warehouse, full of anything you could ever need to raise a kid.

"Thank goodness my almost-stepdaughter Madison is pretty much a teenager," Lola said as they walked through the store. "I won't have to deal with all this stuff."

"No, you just have to deal with sex and drugs." She remembered what it was like being a teenager and shuddered. "I don't envy you."

"Madison's a great kid." A brightness filled Lola's eyes. "She's got a good head on her shoulders."

"You love her," Daniela said, intrigued. She wondered how she'd feel if Nico came with a child. For all she knew, he could have one that she didn't know about. After all, it wasn't as though they really knew each other.

"You're frowning." Lola nudged her.

"I was thinking about someone."

"A man, by the look of it."

"He's all man," she said, her heart beating harder as she remembered how he'd held her. "But I just met him. I don't know anything about him."

"I bet you know more about him than you give yourself credit for." She held her hand out. "Not that there aren't details that you don't know, but details are only that and not super important. Unless he's a criminal or something."

"He's not a serial killer." At Lola's questioning look, she shrugged. "I asked."

Her friend laughed. "What else do you know about him?"

"He owns the world, and he has an empire. He's respected and feared by his colleagues. Very smart and witty." She stopped and studied a stuffed giraffe before moving on. "He's from the wrong side of the tracks, even though he wears custom-made suits now. I get the sense he's kind of a playboy too. He certainly knows his way around a woman's body."

"Fascinating." Nodding absently, Lola stared unseeingly before her. "He sounds like a mix of all the hero archetypes. The chief, the bad boy, the professor, the playboy…"

Daniela smiled at her friend. "I've read all your books, and I still have no idea what you mean."

Lola grinned apologetically. "When you create characters, it helps to have an underlying base guide for him. There are eight basic archetypes, and it sounds like your guy is a little of all of them. But there's got to be one that resonates most with him. Figure that out, and you'll know what appeals to him most."

She nodded, understanding. "I need to figure out his recipe."

"Recipe?"

"My grandmother always said everyone has a recipe, and that to understand the person, you had to know what the ingredients were."

Lola made a face as they entered the clothing department. "You know that sounds hopeless to someone who can't cook, right?"

"Yes, but cooking's my specialty."

"What's my recipe?"

Daniela didn't have to think about it. "Equal parts sugar, laughter, and love, a dash of fairy dust, and a pinch of heat. Slow baked to perfection. Serve in candlelit corners with a sprinkle of salt."

Lola stopped abruptly. "You're dead on."

"I'm good at what I do."

"Your guy doesn't stand a chance, if he's what you really want."

"Maybe." Daniela took a little pink jacket off a rack, but her thoughts were still on Nico. What she *really* wanted was the Harrison building and, based on their last conversation, so did he. She wasn't sure she could have both, in the end.

But that didn't mean she couldn't enjoy him in the meantime.

Her cell phone rang, and her heart leapt when she saw it was Ken. "Lola, I need to answer this."

Her friend nodded. "I'll be over there, drooling over the tutus."

Smiling, Daniela took the call. "Ken? Any word?"

"Yes, and it's not good."

Just as quickly, her heart plummeted. "What happened?"

"Cruz put in an offer higher than yours, also with a deposit. But he put in twenty-percent, which is insane."

She froze, unable to breathe. "What?" she managed to squeak.

"Who does that? It's crazy. The real estate is on prime land, but still." He sighed. "I took the liberty of looking up other properties for you, but I have to tell you, the prospects aren't good. Nothing is as optimal as the Harrison building. You'll have to spend a lot in renovations."

"Make another offer, with a twenty percent deposit." She thought of her bank account and winced. But she could sell her apartment in Paris if she needed. "An make an appointment for me to talk to the owner."

"I'm not sure that'll do any good. Cruz has a far-stretching reach."

"Just do it."

"Consider it done."

"Thank you." She nodded grimly.

"I wish I could offer you more hope, but battling Cruz Enterprises is a losing proposition. Maybe we could—"

"I'll take care of it when I talk to the owner. Thanks, Ken." She hung up and rejoined Lola.

Her friend's brow furrowed. "You don't look happy."

"I'm not. I need a drink." And a knife, to cut out Nico's heart—if he even had one.

"Was it the guy you're interested in?"

Daniela just growled.

Laughing, Lola patted her arm. "Let's pay for this stuff and get you to Eve's so we can pop open the champagne. You can snarl all you want there."

Snarling wasn't going to be enough. She wanted the building—and Nico's head.

The problem was, she wanted his lips, too. And

his hands, and the rest of him. *Still*—even though he was undermining her dream.

Ken was right—it was crazy.

And exhilarating.

She felt the blood coursing through her, pumping her up. Sure she was livid, but she was also eager. Energized. Alive.

Ready.

If Nico wanted a battle, she'd give it to him. She wasn't afraid to fight dirty and, after all, everything was fair.

Chapter Eleven

WHAT WAS HE doing there?

Nico stared at the storefront. There was no sign to indicate what it was. Inside it was dark but, looking into the window, he could see construction materials and debris.

He checked the address again. Jason had assured him this was where her office was located. Jason's research was always unquestionably thorough—it was one of the reasons he was Nico's second-in-command.

Beyond the chaos in front, there was a double door with a light shining from under it. Contractors? Or was Daniela back there? He knocked on the door and waited.

No answer.

He reached for the doorknob and tried it. To his surprise, the door opened. He walked in, carefully making his way to the double doors.

Even before he pushed open the door, he heard Frank Sinatra singing. The air smelled warm and sweet, and he knew without a doubt that Daniela was the one inside.

Excitement surged through him, not unlike when he made his first business conquest. Stronger, though—a potent mix of the hunt and the thrill of victory.

Because he intended to win, the building as well as this game he and Daniela were playing.

Pushing the swinging door, he stood in the entry. The kitchen looked like it was at the end of a remodel. The walls hadn't been painted yet, and there was still plastic covering the cabinet surfaces. After a cursory, professional survey, his attention focused on the main attraction.

She stood at the large island in the center, head bent, rolling what looked like dough. Her hair was piled on her head, but a few curls had escaped, wildly free around her heart-shaped face. The only spot of messiness was a dab of flour on her cheek. Her arms were bare, a white apron the only visible article of clothing.

He thought about her wearing nothing but that utilitarian apron—give or take a pair of heels. He hummed, liking the image. He'd have to make sure that happened.

As an entrepreneur, he was cautious when entering a new partnership. This situation wasn't any different. However, it wasn't a matter of *whether* or *not*. It was *how far did he take it*, and *when did he stop*?

Now was definitely not the time to stop.

He stepped into the kitchen.

Daniela's head popped up, her brow furrowed and barely-leashed fury in her eyes. When she registered who he was, the fury erupted. "You *bastard*. Did you come here to gloat?"

She'd gotten the news, then. He smiled without any humor. "I don't know why I came here."

"Well, you're not welcome." She slammed her fist into the dough. "Unless you've come to say you're sorry."

"No."

"Then get out before I hit you." She brandished the rolling pin at him. "Because you're a jerk. You know how much I want that building and still you're bidding against me."

"Maybe I want it badly, too," he replied mildly, standing across the counter from her.

"You can have any building you want. You don't need that one."

He did, for Eddie, but he wasn't going to get into that.

Daniela glared at him. "You're still here."

"Yes."

Her eyes narrowed, and then before he could react, he was hit on the chest by a blob of dough.

"Sugar cookies are always a crowd pleaser," she said with a satisfied smirk, already rolling another ball in her hand.

He watched, mesmerized by her graceful movements. The urge to have those hands on him surprised him.

Not that he wasn't a physical person. He was, and sex served a purpose. He took care of his needs and was never lacking.

But this yearning was new to him. He normally didn't fantasize about a woman this way, especially one who wanted his balls for another reason other than her own pleasure. Although the way Daniela looked now, he figured cutting off his balls would give her great pleasure.

She lifted the other ball of dough.

"I don't recommend doing that," he warned.

She threw it at him like she was a major league pitcher.

This time, he ducked and charged around the counter. Before she could react, he grabbed her by the waist, turning her around and pinning her against the counter.

"Let me go, damn it." She struggled against him.

"Not until you promise to stop trying to maim me with cookie dough."

"Cookie dough is my secret weapon." She tried to wrestle herself loose.

Her ass wiggled against him, and the feeling shot straight to his head. Unable to help himself, he nuzzled the side of her neck, inhaling her sugary scent. "I think you're wrong about what your secret weapon is."

She growled, but her head tipped to one side. "This isn't going to make me go all docile, you know. I'm not going to just walk away from what I want."

"Good." He placed a kiss there, the lightest brush of his lips, even though he wanted to sink his teeth into her.

Seeing a bowl of melted chocolate in front of them, he dragged his finger in the chocolate and smeared a bit on her exposed neck, licking it clean. "Delicious," he murmured, doing it again.

She arched into him, gasping. "*Nico.*"

"Do you want me to stop?"

"Are you crazy?"

Amazingly, he smiled. Then he smeared another ribbon of chocolate down her neck and then slid his hand under her apron and into her top.

He'd expected her to protest, or to pull away. He was thrilled when she just moaned and rubbed herself against his erection.

He nibbled her skin as his fingers played with her nipple. His other hand trailed down to the waistband of her pants, undid the zipper, and slipped his hand under silky panties.

"I feel like someone should point out that this is a mistake," she said breathlessly.

"Someone probably should," he agreed, "but it's not going to be me."

"Me either." She stretched overhead to tangle her floury fingers in his hair.

He liked it—the messier, the better. He slid his

hand lower into her pants, until his longest finger found what he was looking for.

Her head fell back and she cried out.

His mouth next to her ear, he whispered to her. "I like how open you are to me. You're so wet, and I've barely touched you."

"I have a weakness for bastards."

"Then I'm happy I'm one." He rubbed his finger over the spot that had her panting.

She squirmed in his arms. "I'm not going to be able to hold out."

"I don't want you to. I want to feel you to writhe in my arms. I want you to fall apart. To scream."

She cried out again, and he could feel her losing control of her body. He kept the pressure on her sensitive parts constant, deliberate, knowing by the way she undulated under his touch that the waves of ecstasy were building, ready to crash over her.

"Now, Daniela," he commanded.

And she came—hard and without cease, over and over, calling out his name.

He loved hearing her cry his name.

He held her there, wrapped around her, keeping her grounded and safe, giving her a place to come back to. He was crazy with lust and the need to be inside her. But it was too much, too soon, so when he felt her limbs regain their strength, he righted her clothing and detached himself from her.

As she refastened her hair onto her head, she looked him in the eye. "Don't think that just because you gave me an orgasm that I'm going to stop my bid for the property."

"I'd be disappointed if you did." He adjusted his still very prominent erection to a more comfortable position.

Her eyes fell to his crotch, but then she lifted them again. "You should probably go now."

"I know." He picked up his jacket. Then he went to her, lifted her chin, and kissed her one last time — partly because he wanted to get the last word in and partly because he just needed to.

Smiling at her dazed expression, he strode out, feeling oddly satisfied for someone who was closer to blueballs than any man had ever been.

Chapter Twelve

The house her brother Tony had rented for her was ridiculous. Too big, too grand, and entirely too ostentatious. But it had three ingredients Daniela loved.

The basement. She shuddered, thinking of living down there, but it made Marley happy, and that was all that mattered.

The bathtub in her room. The bathroom itself looked like it belonged in a bordello, with all the red accents and gold fixtures, but the tub was excellent. A modern remake of a deep claw-footed tub, it was perfect for soaking after being on her feet all day.

And the view from the kitchen nook.

Daniela sat there with her coffee and stared out on the trees populating the Presidio. She liked starting her mornings out here — it felt like she was almost in the woods — a unique sensation for a city girl.

This morning, though, instead of seeing the eucalyptus trees edging the back of the house, she just saw Nico's face, flushed with desire.

Wanting her.

She fanned herself. Every time she thought about what they'd done in the showroom kitchen she got hot and bothered all over again. She wasn't sure she'd ever be able to bake in there without remembering how he'd seduced her with his words and his touch.

She'd wanted to be seduced though. Badly, and only by him.

She hadn't heard from Ken regarding the bidding war. Maybe she should make a move on Nico right away, because as soon as one of them bought the building their flirtation would certainly end.

"Daniela, here you are." Marley strode into the kitchen with her briskly efficient walk. "I need to talk to you about a couple things."

She sighed. Marley was a godsend—she couldn't have asked for a better assistant. But sometimes she wanted to tell the young woman to get a life. "Now's not a good time."

"Yes, I can see you're busy."

"Was that sarcasm?" Daniela frowned. "And are

you wearing *pink?*"

The younger woman flushed, touching her sweater defensively. "You bought it for me, and I have black on under it."

She tried to remember the last time Marley had worn anything other than black and drew a blank. "But you never wear anything I give you."

"That's a mistake I'm trying to rectify." Her assistant sat across from her. "We have a couple things we need to discuss. As you know, the clock is ticking down for accepting the Food Network offer. Everyone's eager for your answer."

"No."

Her assistant blinked owlishly at her. "No, they aren't eager?"

"No, I'm not accepting. You know what I mean. Don't play dumb."

Marley took a deep breath, as though she were counting to keep her cool. "Okay, let's talk about Sophie Martineau's birthday party."

"Marley." Daniela leaned forward. "Don't tell me you really want to discuss an aging diva's necessity for status. Because that's all my cake will be to her. She'll order it and coo over it, but she won't even have one bite because she'll worry that it'll add cellulite to her hips and that no amount of lighting will cover it up in her next nude scene."

Her assistant prissied up. "Well, those are the business items we need to take care of."

"Consider them discussed and decided on."

"Daniela—"

Fortunately her cell phone rang right then. She looked at the screen and thanked God it wasn't her brother. "Gotta take this," she said even though the number was blocked. She answered it with "Daniela Rossi."

"Meet me tonight," a dark, earthy voice commanded.

She flushed instantly. "Do you think I'll jump when you tell me to?"

Nico chuckled. "Jumping wasn't what I had in mind, but if you're into that..."

She couldn't help grinning. She probably looked like an idiot, but she really didn't care—not with the prospect of being ravaged by him on the program. "One condition."

"Name it."

"No business, no hidden agendas. This'll only be

about us."

"Deal."

"Seven o'clock," she told him. "Pick me up. I assume since you somehow got my cell phone number you also know where I live."

"I know a whole lot about you, baby, including the way you cry out when you come."

Her face burned hot. Aware of her assistant's curious gaze taking in every detail, she turned away. "Fine. If that's how you want to play it."

"It's definitely how I want to play, Daniela. Seven, sharp." He hung up.

She practically wilted with desire as she set her phone down. What was she going to wear? And, more importantly, what was she going to wear under it?

"Who was that?" Marley asked.

"No one." She pointed at her assistant. "And don't think you'll wheedle the answer out of me. The last thing I need is for Tony to interfere in my personal life."

"You have a personal life?" Marley clapped a hand over her mouth, only her horrified eyes showing. "I'm so sorry. I didn't mean it that way. Of course you have a personal life. I'm just surprised I didn't know about it."

Daniela leaned forward. "If you say a word to Antonio, I'll take away your Justice League."

Marley sat back, gasping. "Harsh."

She nodded, satisfied that she'd made her point.

"This guy must be important," her assistant mused. "Who is he? Do we know he's not after your money?"

She remembered how Ken, her real estate agent, had told her Cruz Enterprises could buy and sell her ten times over, and she collapsed onto the table in a fit of laughter. It wasn't her money Nico was after. It was the Harrison building—and her body. She just wished she knew which he desired more.

"That wasn't really the reaction I expected," she heard Marley mumble.

Shaking her head, Daniela stood up.

"Where are you going?"

"Shopping." She wasn't going to take any chances—she wanted to be prepared for anything tonight. And that meant she needed to make a stop at Romantic Notions.

On impulse, she called Eve and had her meet her

at the lingerie store, since Eve and Olivia, the woman who owned the shop, were good friends.

Eve was in the store, talking to a very pregnant Olivia, when Daniela arrived. Both women turned to her eagerly, but Eve was the one who said, "Who is he?"

She didn't pretend to play coy. "No one. Yet."

"But you want him to be," Eve said.

Olivia nodded. "We can help with that."

"He's direct and to the point." Daniela looked around, smiling distractedly at the young woman behind the counter—Olivia's new hire, Nicole, according to Eve. "I don't know if he's not into the trappings of romance, if you know what I mean."

"All men are into trappings. You just have to find the right trigger. Something simple that'll showcase the goods, I think." Olivia surveyed the store from her perch. Then she turned to Nicole. "What do you think?"

"The red," she said without hesitation.

Olivia smiled proudly. "Exactly."

"I'll get it." The young woman rushed behind the curtain, presumably to the backroom.

"I'm training her to mostly run the store while I'm

on leave with the baby," Olivia said. "I think she's going to be great. She's got the right instincts."

Nicole returned holding out a red bra and matching panties. "Want to try it on?"

Daniela looked at Olivia. "Do I need to?"

She shook her head. "It's going to be perfect."

"Okay then." She handed her credit card over. "Let's do it."

Eve leaned her hips against the counter. "You know we expect details, right?"

"If you wear that"—Olivia pointed to the underwear Nicole was bagging up—"the details are going to be juicy."

Daniela grinned. She hoped so. She really did.

At six fifty-nine, Daniela stepped outside, right as Nico rolled to a stop in front of the house. His slinky car purred as it idled.

She slid inside, taking him in. He wore slacks and an immaculate dress shirt with a couple buttons undone.

Flushed with the urge to kiss that bared patch of skin at his collar, she fanned herself.

"Warm?" he asked, adjusting the vents.

Overheated by testosterone was more like it. She felt like she was drowning in it. But it'd be a happy way to go. She tucked the black lace of her dress around her legs. "My brother would approve of your ride."

"I approve of your dress."

"Thank you." She loved this dress. It was vintage, from the fifties, and made her feel like a movie star. More importantly, it made Nico look at her like she was good enough to eat.

But wait till he saw what was underneath. With a secret smile, she buckled herself in. "Where are we going?"

"My place."

She glanced at his profile as he eased the car from the curb. "Is that a good idea?"

"It's a *great* idea." He flashed her a wolfish grin.

She hid her smile by looking out the window. Tonight was a great idea. Soon they'd have an answer on the building, and then who knew —

No thoughts about business, she told herself. She was going to revel in Nico tonight. What happen from here on out was up to Fate and him.

They drove in silence, which was a first for her. Normally she was chatty, especially when she was nervous or unsure. Talking made her feel bold.

She wasn't nervous, though, she realized. Yes, she had butterflies, but they were from anticipation rather than anxiety.

He pulled to a stop at the curb in front of a curved walkway. She read the sign on the building. The Mandarin Oriental.

A valet came around the car and opened the door as Nico put the car in park. "Good evening, Mr. Cruz."

"Robin." Nico unbuckled his seat belt and got out. "Did you send in your application to Berkeley?"

"Yes, sir." The valet beamed at him. "Thanks again for the recommendation."

Interesting, she thought as she pried herself out of the low car. She watched Nico hand the boy what looked like an impressive tip before coming to escort her inside.

"I thought we were going to your place," she said as he escorted her through the lobby.

"We are."

"But only people on nighttime TV dramas live in

hotels."

"It suits me." He swiped a card on the elevator keypad. The doors closed and they shot up to the top floor. The doors swooshed open directly into his suite.

She walked in, awestruck. She wasn't a stranger to luxury—she'd been in some of the most ostentatious homes and castles around the world. But to live in a hotel suite like this cost a small fortune. If he could afford to spend money on this, her project was doomed. She had money, but not like this.

Now wasn't the time to dwell on that. No business—only pleasure.

Pushing away the worry, she strode to the wall of windows that looked out on half of San Francisco, from the Bay Bridge to the Golden Gate and in between. "This is amazing. No wonder you live here."

He came to stand behind her, his hand on the small of her back. "I live here because it's convenient. The view is a bonus."

"You're lying." She glanced over her shoulder at him. "The view is why you live here. Otherwise you'd have converted one of the floors of your office building into a living space. Here, you sit on top of the city."

"Most people wouldn't have the guts to call me a liar, even if they were thinking it," he said too casually.

"Guts have never been something I lacked."

He smiled, his hand tightening on her waist. "Wine?"

She turned around. "You."

A predatory look darkened his gaze. He walked her back until she was pressed against the cold sheet of glass. "I thought we'd have dinner first."

Goose bumps broke out up and down her body, as much from his hands on her as the chill of the glass. Her heart began to pound with the promise of the chase. "Let's start with dessert."

"I like dessert." He lightly rasped his chin against her neck.

"So do I," she said as he slipped a hand up her leg and under her dress.

She hummed as his hand ran all the way up the back of her leg. It didn't stop until his fingers found the edge of her lacy new underwear.

"Do you rip the wrapping off your presents?" she asked as she nuzzled his neck where his shirt opened at the collar. "Or do you enjoy the wrapping just as much as what's underneath?"

"What do you think?"

"I think you should take the time to appreciate the wrapping once in a while."

He lifted his head and looked at her with that enigmatic gaze. Then he turned her around.

She frowned, her hands bracing on the glass. "What are you doing?"

"Unwrapping my present," he whispered in her ear as he unzipped the back of her dress. "Slowly."

The lace gave way, loosening at the top and then all the way down to her hips. Nico's hands slid under the straps and dragged them down her arms. She shimmied her arms out to help him.

Her dress fell to the floor.

She stepped out of it and kicked it aside, so she stood there in her heels and the new red number.

There was silence behind her. She saw his reflection in the window, staring at her body like it was the most incredible thing he'd ever seen.

He ran a hand over her curves and then tugged on the thong. "Who makes this? I want to buy stock in the company."

She chuckled and then turned around. Grabbing

his shirt, she tugged him closer and began unbuttoning. "Your turn."

She slowly undid his shirt, pulling it out of his pants, running her hands over his taut chest. He was muscular, the kind that was more like a construction worker than a pampered executive. His skin was tanned, like the perfect latte.

"When I was a kid, on Christmas my brother would always complain because I took too long opening my presents. The exterior delighted me as much as what was inside." She smiled up at Nico. "I may have been a little slower just to annoy him though."

"You and your brother are close."

Her humor faded, and she dropped her gaze to his chest. Instead of answering, she shrugged, and then she kissed his chest, to distract them both. Because she liked it, she did it again.

His hands gathered in her hair and he pulled her close. Lifting her head, she got on her toes and brought his mouth down to hers as she unbuckled his belt and slid her hand in. Her eyes widened when her fingers met naked, hard, silky flesh. "You *do* go commando."

He hummed deep in his throat, pressing her

closer, his fingers sliding under her lace panties.

The tip of his longest finger grazed her sex, the faintest brush that had her panting, just like the last time. She unzipped his pants and shoved them down. He kicked off his shoes and, with her help, his socks and everything else.

They stood and stared at each other, admiring.

Wanting.

And then he picked her up and carried her to the couch, sitting so that she straddled his hips on top.

"We can get rid of this." He unhooked her bra and tossed it aside. "I've admired my present long enough, I think."

"I think so too." She wiggled out of her underwear and tossed that aside, too.

Suddenly he held a condom—she had no idea where it came from, but she put her hand out. "Let me."

He handed it over silently and sat back, arms folded behind his head, watching her with so much desire it made her breath catch.

She ripped the wrapper off and slowly sheathed him, taking her time, knowing it was driving him crazy. Her hands caressed all of him in the process, until his hips were arching up and he groaned in need.

Then his hands grabbed her and settled her on top. His gaze was glittery with need, his jaw tight like his control was almost at an end. "You're playing with me."

"And you like it."

He growled as he rolled over so she was on the bottom. "We'll see how much you like."

She arched as his mouth trailed down her torso. "That sounded like a threat."

His hands pushed her thighs open. "I don't threaten, baby. I just do," he promised as he lowered his head.

And then he *did*—with his mouth and fingers, until she was writhing uncontrollably on the leather. Just when she thought she couldn't take anymore, he focused on the one most sensitive spot and sucked gently.

She screeched, gripping his head, coming off the couch.

Without pause, he shifted and slid inside her to the hilt. Two thrusts and she came again, her cries swallowed by his kisses. She gripped him closer, wrapping her legs around his waist, urging him faster.

He didn't take much urging. Moments later he groaned in orgasm himself, arching up, his face taut with ecstasy.

Then he lowered himself on top of her.

They lay there, sweaty, for a long time. Then she said, "I'm a big fan of having dessert before dinner."

He ran a hand over her hip and down her thigh. "I could tell."

"But that doesn't mean we shouldn't have dessert after dinner, too."

"You're already thinking to the next time?"

"Of course." She smiled innocently at him. "I have a sweet tooth."

Chapter Thirteen

MARLEY CROUCHED IN the doorway to the main kitchen in their house, peering around the corner to see Daniela in an overlarge man's shirt, barefoot and seemingly naked underneath, whisking something in a bowl.

Her boss was *singing*.

It wouldn't have been an unusual occurrence a year ago. But since before they'd moved to San Francisco, Marley would have been able to count on one hand the number of times she'd caught Daniela singing. She'd have been able to count on one hand even if she'd had both her hands amputated.

She ducked as Daniela danced around the corner and did a little two-step to Bing Crosby's White Christmas.

Singing. Cooking without clothes on. Strange phone calls. Not coming home until really early in the morning.

Brian was right: there was a man in this scenario.

Her cell phone rang. Cursing under her breath, she crawled backwards, away from the kitchen so her boss wouldn't catch her. She looked at the screen and, answered, whispering, "Brian, how did you know?"

"Know what?"

"That Daniela was seeing someone."

"Marley, do you have laryngitis?"

"No." She almost dropped the phone as she continued to crawl down the hallway, so Daniela wouldn't hear her. "I'm being stealthy."

"Oh." Then he whispered back, "Why?"

"Because I was peeking in on my boss."

"You mean you were spying."

"No, I was definitely only peeking." She frowned. "Why are you calling? Because obviously it's not to gloat over knowing she was seeing someone."

"I want to go to the Ferry Building. The farmers market is this morning."

"That's nice. Have a good time."

"Okay. I'll pick you up in fifteen."

"What?" She made a face. "*No.* I'm not going."

"What else are you going to do on such a beautiful Saturday morning? Spy on your boss? Read comic books? *Work?*"

"You say that like it's a curse."

"It's probably the nicest Saturday we're going to have in a long time, and you're passing up a ride on my bike to people watch and eat bad-for-you things from street vendors. But, hey, to each his own."

She rolled her eyes. But the ride on the bike was tempting, and the last time she'd gone to the Ferry Building it'd been with Daniela, and she'd *really* wished she'd had her camera. What was a culinary treat for most people was a visual treat for her. The thought of taking photos excited her. She hadn't taken any pictures in so long. "Twenty minutes," she said impulsively.

"You got it." He hung up, probably so she couldn't change her mind.

Scrambling to her feet, she hurried downstairs. On impulse, she put on a pair of jeans and a turquoise blue long-sleeved shirt with beading—also a gift from Daniela. She topped it with a gray blazer, a scarf, and her camera bag.

She let herself out of her Batcave right as Brian drove up. He rolled up the driveway and stopped in front of her. She was momentarily struck speechless by the look of him. He looked *badass*.

Afraid to blurt out what she was thinking, she wordlessly took the helmet he offered, jammed it on her head, and hopped on. He turned around in the driveway and they roared off.

A thrill of excitement rushed through her. She held him tightly around his waist, even though she felt comfortable this time. She liked the solid feel of him against the front of her body.

She gasped at the thought, feeling guilty like she'd been unfaithful to Tony. She quickly erased it from her mind, as if he'd know.

Marley hopped off before Brian backed into a spot between two cars and parked the motorcycle. Undoing her helmet, she handed it to him.

He secured both helmets to the bike and then took her hand. "Let's go."

She followed, staring down at their linked hands. It felt... weird. Not bad, just weird. It was kind of nice, actually, in a way. Not awkward, like she'd have expected it to be.

"Uh-oh." A smile threatened his lips as he led her across the Embarcadero. "You're thinking. That can't result in anything good. Let me assure you that this is platonic."

"My friends don't usually hold my hand."

"Then you need better friends."

"Actually, I was trying to remember the last time I held anyone's hand."

"Do you remember the first time?"

She looked at him incredulously. "Do you?"

"Of course." He looked at her like she was silly. "Kindergarten. Mary Ellen Fisher. She had two blond braids and buck teeth."

Marley laughed.

"I loved her teeth. It broke my heart when she got braces in sixth grade." He shot her a grin. "Your turn."

She couldn't remember the first time. She couldn't even remember her mother holding it. She *did* remember one time when Tony had put his hand on hers—it'd lasted only a second, but she couldn't bring herself to wash that hand all day. "I don't think anyone held my hand in school."

"What about after? What about your One True Love, the guy you're waiting for?"

She tried to imagine Tony holding someone's

hand and just couldn't see it. "I don't think he's that type, and other guys always saw me as another one of them."

Brian looked her up and down, a disbelieving look on his face. "Whatever you need to tell yourself. Come on. This stand over here has the best squash."

"Squash?" She wrinkled her nose.

"Wait till you see them. Close your eyes."

"Brian, that's just—"

"No, really. Trust me." He stared at her steadily, waiting.

Sighing, she closed her eyes. She wanted to say that she was humoring him, but she did trust him.

He slowly, carefully guided her for what seemed like forever before telling her to stop. "Open your eyes."

Blinking, she focused on an amazing array of oranges, greens, yellows, and whites. All shapes and sizes, it was more like an art exhibit than a squash stand.

"See." He poked her. "I wouldn't steer you wrong."

Enchanted by the colors, she pulled out her camera and began to take pictures, appreciating that Brian stood out of the way and patiently let her do her thing. She took close-ups and shots at a distance, photos of the merchant holding a long squash suggestively, and of a patron laughing. Inspired, she changed the aperture and did a long-exposure still with people moving in the background to create a blur.

Then she tossed a squat orange squash to Brian. "Kiss it."

"*Kiss it?*" He made sour a face at the squash.

She snapped the picture, grinning. "It might turn into the princess you've always been waiting for."

"I haven't always been waiting for a princess."

She snapped another, changing angles.

"And an inanimate object like a squash can't turn into a princess," he added with feigned superiority. "Someone like you should know that."

She took another photo. "Someone like me?"

"Smart. More than book smart." He studied her, as if looking for the right word, and she caught it with her camera. "Wise beyond her years."

She lowered it. "Please don't tell me you're calling me old."

"How old are you?"

"Twenty-nine."

"I'm thirty. I beat you." He took her hand and dragged her away. "Since you're taking pictures, let's go down the Embarcadero. Have you had any photo shoots by the arrow?"

"What arrow?"

He shook his head. "You're practically still a tourist rather than a resident, aren't you? Don't worry, we'll take care of some of the essentials today."

He led her down the piers toward the Bay Bridge, filling her in on history tidbits and pointing out hot spots, like the pier where he had his first kiss. She shook her head and caught his antics with her camera.

She also took pictures of other people walking by. She got a young couple to pose by the huge silver rocket ship, and caught the first steps of a baby who decided it was time to step out on her own as well as the parents' amazement.

After a little while, Brian said, "Let's walk up this pier. There's a bench at the end."

"Where you lost your virginity?" she asked with a little sarcasm.

"No. I lost my virginity in the backseat of my friend's classic Cadillac." He grinned at her. "It was green."

"I hope you mean the car."

"I can't imagine what else you'd think would be green." He sat down on the bench and stretched an arm on the backrest, leaving a space open for her to slide in.

She sat, stiff, aware of him so close. *Leaning.* His fingers played with the ends of her hair.

The bridge was behind him, the light was just right, and he had a contented look on his face. She took a picture of it to distract herself from the feel of him next to her.

"Give me that." He held his hand out.

"My camera?"

"No, your bra."

She gave him a baleful look.

"Of course, your camera." He grinned. "Unless handing over your bra would actually be a possibility."

"In your dreams," she said as she changed the setting to automatic and handed over the Nikon.

"Every night." He pointed it at her and looked through the lens. "Make love to the camera."

"Right."

He snapped a picture. "You're a sexy, sexy tiger. Growl for me, baby."

She laughed.

He took another photo. Then he leaned in, so his head was against hers, and took one of the two of them.

Still laughing, she turned her head.

And suddenly his lips were on hers.

She went still, frozen with shock.

His mouth was the only thing that touched her, and it was so gentle, so unthreatening, that it coaxed her into responding.

Where most guys would have taken that as a green light to go, Brian didn't change the pace at all. He urged her along slowly, without any demands, a brush of his tongue, a nibble of his lips. Warm and moist.

Skillful. He knew what he was doing.

There was nothing innocuous about it, though. He wasn't touching her, but she could feel the pull of it throughout her body, pooling molten right at the center of her.

He angled his head and deepened it for just a moment before he shifted away. Marley blinked, stunned by all of it, vaguely aware of him taking one more photo.

"Come on." He stood up and held out his hand. "Let's get gelato in the Ferry Building. You can take more pictures in there."

"Okay," she said faintly, dazedly standing up. Then she realized she didn't have her camera.

As if reading her mind, Brian said, "I'll give it back to you when I'm sure you won't drop it."

"Fair enough," she muttered.

He smiled and took her hand, twining his fingers through hers. She looked down at their entangled hands, deciding that she liked it.

She liked it a lot.

Chapter Fourteen

Daniela looked at the loaves of cinnamon bread lining the counter. How many should she take with her?

Her real estate agent had come through and gotten her a meeting with the man who owned the building. According to Ken, the man's father had left him the building as part of an inheritance and he had no interest in it. She was supposed to meet him in—she checked the time—an hour, and she didn't intend to go empty handed.

Nor did she expect to come back without the building owner promising to sell her the property.

There was only one sticky point: Nico.

She was about to undermine him. She rationalized it by telling herself he could buy any building for his project—she didn't have that luxury. None of the other properties Ken had showed her were viable. Either they were too far out of the city proper or required so much remodel that she may as well just built something from the ground up.

Which meant she had to convince the owner to sell it to her, even if she had to deliver a cake in the shape of a pirate ship to him every week (she'd made one for Johnny Depp once).

Would Nico still want to see her after the building was hers? The male ego was such a delicate thing. If this thing between them were just sex, buying the building wouldn't be a problem. They'd get it on a couple more times and then call it quits.

But she had a feeling this wasn't just sex. It felt like more. Much more.

She thought about the last time, at his hotel suite. They hadn't burned out all night, until she finally asked him to return her home at five in the morning. He'd wanted her to stay the night, but he hadn't argued when she said she wanted to go.

She'd needed to leave. She'd needed space. It'd been too intense. She'd left so quickly she forgot her underwear.

Marley cleared her throat. "You've been baking a lot lately."

She startled, having forgotten her assistant was there. Sometimes Marley was like a mouse, shuffling quietly around the house, running in the shadows.

"It's funny, though," Marley said in an offhand tone that wasn't really offhand at all. "We haven't had any pastries around the house."

"That's funny?"

"It's certainly odd. It makes me wonder where the pastries are going." She shrugged, tapping into her ever-present phone. "If, for instance, you have a black market supply chain for gingerbread men."

Not ready to discuss her plans with anyone, Daniela took the offense. "What's going on with you?"

Marley blinked, looking startled. "What do you mean?"

"You've been strange lately. More so than usual."

"Thanks." She rolled her eyes and refocused on her phone.

"I mean it. You've been outspoken, and you look different." Daniela looked more closely, snapping her fingers as she realized what was off. "You're wearing color, and your hair is down."

Blushing, Marley tucked her hair behind her ear. "It's not a crime to leave your hair down."

"No, but it's out of character." She leaned on the counter. "Are you sick?"

"No."

"In love?"

"*No.*" Marley glared at her. "That's just ridiculous."

But something in the way Marley protested caught her attention. Daniela just hoped the sudden changes were inspired by a man other than her brother, because Antonio Rossi was a selfish bastard. In her unbiased opinion, anyway.

"If you really want to know what's going on with me," her assistant began coyly, "I can tell you."

She threw her arms in the air. "Finally! Thank you. Just stop dancing around it and let me know what's going on."

Marley leaned forward, her gaze like a laser. "The Food Network."

Daniela groaned.

"I don't understand your reluctance to do this." Marley shook her head. "It'd be great for your career."

It would, if she still wanted her career.

"It'd make your brother happy, too," her assistant

offered.

"Exactly," she said darkly. He'd been harassing her more and more, and she was sick of it. Not once did he ask her how *she* was doing—it was always about work. She grabbed a couple plastic bags and twist ties and began wrapping up the loaves. She'd take three.

Of course, Marley didn't hear the sarcasm. "So you agree?"

"Of course I don't." She viciously twisted the end of the plastic bag closed.

"Why not? I don't understand. The last time you were so excited to do it."

"My focus has changed. I'm growing in a different direction."

Marley fiddled nervously with her phone. "What do I tell Tony?"

"Tell him whatever you want. He's not my favorite right now. He'll be lucky if I even buy him coal for Christmas this year." It shouldn't surprise him. She'd replied to his last email with *Feel free to jump off the Brooklyn Bridge*. He probably understood the subtext, that she was pissed with him. He was perceptive that way. "I need to go. I'll see you later."

Before Marley could start talking about Sophie Martineau, who was also harassing her, or some other detail that she probably should have been paying attention to but couldn't care less about, she ran up all the stairs to her tower room to change.

She got ready in record time, called a cab, collected the bread, and went outside to wait. It was time to focus.

Daniela had asked Ken for intel, and he'd produced a good amount of information. She was on her way to meet Chris Ludlow, community college science teacher who wanted to pay off the massive loans he'd taken out for his two kids' college tuition.

She had the taxi driver take her to the coffeehouse in the Mission where Chris suggested they meet. Carrying her loaves, she strode into the café and looked around.

She knew him instantly. He sat in a high-backed chair in the corner, quietly watching the world through his thick lenses. His hair was thin on the top, but he hadn't combed it over like so many men's egos dictated they do. He glanced at her, perking up when he saw her.

She knew he recognized her. It was always obvious. Usually she hated it, but in this case she planned to use it to her full advantage. She smiled brightly and strode to him. "Chris?"

"Yes." He half got up.

"No, please sit." She set the bread on the table in front of him and shook his hand. "I'm Daniela."

"Daniela Rossi," he said, dazed, staring at her in wonder. "My wife watches your show."

"The reruns now." She sat across from him, unwinding the scarf from her neck.

"She's been watching for years. It baffles me, but she loves to try to copy your recipes." He leaned closer conspiratorially. "She's a god-awful cook."

Grinning, she pushed the bread closer to him. "Then maybe you can both enjoy this."

He looked inside the bag, blinked, and then gaped at her. "Did you make these?"

"Of course."

"Then there's no way Tillie will let me eat any of it," he said mournfully. "She'll want to bronze them and mount them on the wall."

"Take her one and hide the other two for yourself." Daniela winked at him.

He burst into laughter. "You're as spunky as you

are on TV. I like you."

Chris insisted on getting her a tea, and then they chatted about his job at City College, and his sons, and how his wife had been trying different ways of keeping herself busy since their youngest went to college. Currently, she was trying knitting, which he said was only somewhat better than her attempts at cooking.

Daniela had planned on being charming, but she found she didn't need to be. She enjoyed chatting with him. She even told him what she wanted the building for.

She hadn't told anyone—not even Ken in any great detail—about her plans for starting a soup kitchen and apprentice shop. He listened to her impassioned plans silently.

At the end, he nodded. "My wife would love that."

Leaning forward, she pressed. "In addition to the soup kitchen, I'm thinking of offering classes, too. Cooking and other vocational skills that'd be useful."

He looked at the bread.

Feeling like a shoulder devil, she pushed the bag closer to him. "Try a piece. I cut a few slices on one of the loaves."

He opened the bag and searched for the cut loaf. He ceremoniously untwisted the tie, took a thick piece, and bit into it. His face flushed as he chewed. "This is delicious," he whispered reverently when he could talk.

Smiling, she sat back and waited, knowing she'd said everything she'd needed to. The rest was up to him.

He brushed the crumbs from his lap. "You know we have the recent higher offer from Cruz Enterprises."

"Yes." The bastard kept outbidding her. "I'm prepared to meet it, and I can put down twenty-percent to guarantee the offer."

"I was surprised that there was so much instant interest in the building." Chris shook his head as he reached for another slice. "It'd be great to close the deal by Christmas."

"I'm fully prepared to do that."

"Well, I know my wife would like something going in there that was useful to society. Plus, like I said, she's a big fan of yours." He nodded. "So the building is yours. I'll call my real estate guy and let him know."

She held her breath, afraid she'd heard wrong. "Are you sure?"

"Yes." He held his hand out to shake on it, but she stood and hugged him, tears of happiness flooding her eyes. "Thank you," she said, squeezing him.

He patted her back awkwardly. "Do good."

She left on cloud nine. She was in a cab when Ken called her.

"I don't know what you said to him, but it worked," he told her. "I just got a call from his agent asking for us to resubmit a formal offer with twenty-percent, and that they'd accept it."

"I told you I could do it," she said smugly.

"Go celebrate. I'll fax you the paperwork to sign."

She hung up, tapping her foot against the front passenger seat. The only person she felt like celebrating with was one who wasn't going to be as happy about her purchase. But she called him anyway.

He answered on the second ring. "Cruz."

"I know you're holding my underwear hostage," she said in greeting.

"I feel confident we can come to some sort of arrangement."

"I'm sure we can. What are you doing now?"

Sweet on You

"Imagining stripping you naked."

She shivered. "That's not why I called, but I like it nonetheless."

"Why did you call?"

"You won't like it," she said gleefully.

"Tell me anyway."

"When I get there. If you're free."

"For you? Come now."

"I want to," she purred.

"Then I'll see you at my suite."

She hung up and told the driver to reroute to the Mandarin Oriental.

Apparently, the staff had been alerted to her arrival. An official man in hotel livery whisked her from the taxi to the elevator and up to Nico's suite. She thanked her escort and walked into the living area.

Nico sat on the couch, in suit pants and a dress shirt with the sleeves rolled up. His bare feet were oddly sexy, as was the hawk-like expression on his face as he read whatever document was in his hands.

He looked up when she walked in.

"I won the building," she said without preamble. She dropped her purse and outer layers on a table and went to stand directly in front of him, her hip kicked out saucily. "I convinced the owner to sell it to me."

He set his papers aside and stood. "Well done."

Some of her joy faded under confusion. "You're not angry?"

"Because you went for what you wanted? No. I'm proud of you." He stepped up to her and smoothed back her hair. "But you haven't signed papers yet."

"He agreed to sell it to me, and he's a good guy." She arched her neck.

He obliged her by kissing it. "Except I don't lose, and I really want that building."

She closed her eyes. "Are you going to be a sore loser?"

"Baby, I haven't lost yet." He grabbed her close, slipping his hand under her top, and unhooking her bra in one sexy motion. "And I don't plan on losing. Ever."

She opened her mouth to tell him there was always a first time, but he kissed her. And then kissed her some more. And then she forgot everything but the feel of his mouth on her and the touch of his hands.

Chapter Fifteen

MARLEY HAD TWO choices: stick around and talk to Tony, who was supposed to call for a phone conference in ten minutes, or make herself unavailable.

Second option—without a doubt. She couldn't talk to Tony. She was afraid she might tell him about Daniela, and she wasn't sure how to handle that yet. So she grabbed the present for Valentine, left her cell phone, and walked out of the house.

It hadn't occurred to her that Valentine might not be in her office until she was halfway there, but she shouldn't have worried, because the matchmaker sat on her gilded couch, fiddling with her iPhone.

Valentine looked up with a bright smile as Marley walked in. "I was just thinking about you. You saved me a phone call."

"Did you need something?"

"I just wondered how you were doing." She wrinkled her nose. "What do you have in your hand?"

"Oh." Marley looked down at the package, suddenly having doubts. "It's not really anything. I just thought you might like it, but—"

"I love gifts. Let me see." Valentine held her hand out.

She handed it over reluctantly. "It's really nothing great. In fact, it's not that nice."

"Let me be the judge of that." She ripped off the wrapping, tossing the shredded pieces of paper all over so that Marley started to bend over to pick them up.

Until Valentine's gasp startled her back upright. "What is it?"

"This. Is. *Amazing*." Valentine stared at the framed photo, her big eyes wider than usual.

Some of her nerves receded, and Marley sat down on the uncomfortable chair across from the matchmaker. "It's not the best composition, but I thought you looked nice in it."

"Nice? I look *awesome*." Valentine stared at the photo. It was the one Marley took that day when she'd been in answering those random questions that had matched her up with Brian Benedict.

Who was plaguing her, by the way. Marley shifted on the seat, uncomfortable and not sure what to do—about her butt or the guy. "It's really not anything—"

"It's the best picture anyone's ever taken of me." Valentine hugged it to her chest, beaming. "I wish I had a boyfriend to give it to."

"You don't have a boyfriend?"

"It's like the cobbler's kids not having shoes." She set the framed picture on the coffee table in front of her. "I don't have time to look for myself. I'm trying to get my business off the ground. Which is why I'm glad you're here. Tell me about Brian."

Marley crossed her arms. "What about him?"

"Brian told me that you guys were going out but not dating."

"Does that violate the terms of my agreement with you?"

"I don't care about our agreement," Valentine said in her schoolmarm's voice. "I care about you messing this up with Brian. He's the perfect guy for you."

But she'd always thought Tony was The One. "How can you tell?"

"What are you talking about?" She shook her

head. "How can you not tell?"

"I've always wanted Batman."

The redhead gaped at her.

Marley blushed. "I know it's ridiculous, but I've always had a thing for Batman. I *dream* about him. He bursts through my window and coaxes me out into the night, taking me on adventures through the city."

Leaning in, Valentine said, "You know Batman is fictional, right? He doesn't really exist."

No, but Tony did, and usually in her dreams, it was Tony in the batsuit.

Until last night. Last night, she dreamt about Brian Benedict.

"Okay, Marley, let's just get this straight." She leaned in. "I match people up for a living. It's what I do best, so when I say you and Brian are perfect together, I don't mean it lightly."

"But I'm in love with someone else."

"What?" Valentine's face screwed up. "Who? Batman?"

"No." She tried to think of how to describe Tony. "Someone I used to know in New York."

"Why didn't you tell me? Does he love you?"

Only when she wrangled Daniela in the direction

he wanted. She shrugged. "We've never had any conversation discussing that."

Valentine deflated with relief. "Okay, then."

"I told Brian, too. He knows I have feelings for someone else."

"He does? So you two have never kissed?"

She flushed instantly.

Valentine waved at her face. "What does that guilty expression mean?"

"We may have kissed." She rushed on to say, "But it was just friendly."

"Really."

"Did Brian tell you something different?"

"He didn't tell me about any kiss."

Damn it. She made a face or something. "That's because it was no big deal."

"Sort of like friendly fire that isn't a big deal?" Valentine stared at her for a long, silent moment. Then she leaned forward. "Just to clarify one more time, you realize I'm a matchmaker, right? I hook people up for a living."

"Yes." Now wasn't the time to point out that Valentine had enlisted her because she'd needed help in growing her business.

"So when I say you and Brian would be good together, it shouldn't be taken lightly. I put some thought into it, and you guys would be terrific together."

"Why?" she asked impulsively.

"Why?" Valentine blinked at her. "Was the kiss awful?"

The kiss was pretty damn terrific, but she didn't think she should arm the matchmaker with ammunition. "It was fine."

Valentine narrowed her eyes, as if trying to see within her. Finally she said, "You need to respect my skills. I wouldn't have paired you up with a loser. I have too much at stake here. So if you have any interest in yourself, it'd behoove you to take this seriously and go out with Brian on a real date."

Marley blinked in shock. She didn't want to date Brian Benedict—not entirely, anyway. Part of her clung to the idea of Tony. She thought about him, recalling his eyes. They were a beautiful gray-blue—

No—Brian's eyes were gray. Tony had brown eyes, like Daniela.

She wanted to slap her forehead.

Valentine sat back, folding her hands properly

in her lap, seemingly innocent. But her expression gave away the unyielding adamantium underneath. "Don't screw this up. It could be the best thing that ever happened to you."

Marley wasn't sure about that. The problem was, she couldn't argue against it either.

Chapter Sixteen

TYING THE LAST ribbon on the last present, Daniela sat crossed-legged on the living room floor and looked at her handiwork with satisfaction. The pile of brightly wrapped boxes was impressive. She figured she'd gone a little overboard, buying things for her homeless family. But most of the items were useful—underwear and warm layers. The only frivolous items were a doll and a football. She hadn't been able to help herself.

She couldn't wait to deliver everything. If only she could be there to watch them open the presents.

Her phone rang. That was all it ever did these days. It seemed like she was constantly answering someone's call.

Who would it be this time? Sophie Martineau again, begging her for a birthday cake? Her brother?

Someone else wanting a piece of her? Dispassionately, she glanced at the screen.

Ken, her real estate person. Perking up, she answered. "Tell me my contract is in the mail."

"That's exactly why I'm calling." He paused.

His silence didn't bode well. "What happened?"

"There's a hold up on the other end. I'm trying to unravel what's taking so long."

"There's no problem, is there?"

"No. Ludlow's real estate agent hasn't returned my calls. He's probably out of town. He's an avid skier. He has a ski house in Tahoe, and he goes up there as often as he can."

"You don't sound certain," she said, standing up. "I can hear the doubt in your voice."

"Any delay bothers me, but especially in this case, since Cruz Enterprises expressed such a strong desire for the Harrison building as well."

"Don't worry about Cruz Enterprises." Nico could desire the building all he wanted, but she'd gotten Chris Ludlow's word, and she knew the man would honor it. His wife wouldn't let him live it down, otherwise.

"I don't know how you can be so sure," Ken was

saying, "but I'll trust you."

"Just work on getting the paperwork finalized," she told him.

"Will do. I'll hopefully call you with good news soon."

"Thanks, Ken." As she hung up another call came in—Tony.

She did *not* want to talk to her brother. Except in ending the call with Ken and trying to ignore Tony, she pressed the wrong button and accepted his call.

Damn it. She glared at his cocky smile on her screen and put the phone to her ear. "I don't want to talk to you."

"That's too bad, because you have to."

Her hackles rose. "I don't have to do anything," she retorted, knowing she sounded like herself at twelve and not caring.

"Stop acting like a child and listen, Daniela. We have business to discuss."

"No."

He heaved a sighed. Then, in a pseudo-calm voice, he said, "I know you were overworked, but you've had several weeks of downtime to recuperate. It's time to get back into the game."

"It's Christmastime," she pointed out archly.

"So?"

She held the phone out and gaped at it. Then she returned it to her ear. "Who are you? Did you hear what you just said? I never work at Christmas."

"You did last year."

Last year she'd needed to work. Nonna had just died, and she'd been brokenhearted. It made her furious—and sad—that her brother didn't get that.

"And there's no reason not to work this year," he continued, oblivious. "You don't have any other plans."

"How would you know?"

"Do you?" he asked with exaggerated patience.

"I have *tons* of plans." She narrowed her eyes. "In fact, I'm buying a building."

"What building? To do what?"

"To open a soup kitchen."

"*What?*"

"And a homeless shelter," she added with grim delight.

"The hell you are."

"Oh, I really am, Antonio. I've got it all outlined. I'm going to offer housing and food, and even cooking classes," she added, proud. "To help people find a vocation and get back on their feet."

"You're *insane*." There was a scuffle of noise on the other end. "You aren't the type of person to direct this sort of operation. It requires organization and business skills."

"So?"

"So, you bake cookies."

She gasped. "You bastard."

"I didn't mean it like that, and you know it. You're excellent at what you do, and what you do is baking. You don't know the first thing about running a charity. For instance, how are you fundraising?"

"I'm not." She lifted her chin defiantly, even though he wasn't there to see it. "I have plenty of money on my own."

"See? That's what I'm talking about. That's just foolish." He paused and took a deep breath, as though trying to calm himself. "Listen to me, Daniela, starting a soup kitchen is the last thing you should be doing. You just don't have the skills."

She hung up, feeling her blood boiling in her veins. She began to pace, but it didn't help so she picked up a vase from the mantle and heaved it across the room. It hit the wall and shattered into a shower of tiny shards.

Marley rushed into the living room, out of breath and looking uncharacteristically disheveled. "What happened?"

"It slipped." Daniela shrugged. "At least it was empty."

"Hmm." Her assistant frowned at the mess on the floor. "I hope it's not me you're angry at."

"No, and I'm no longer angry at anyone." She flashed a grim smile. "I just needed to express."

Marley watched her cautiously. "Have you expressed it all out of your system, or do I need to be prepared to duck?"

"It's always good to be prepared." She tossed her hair over her shoulder and went to do that herself. She'd show Tony. She'd show everyone. She could accomplish anything she set her mind to doing—and that included outbidding a real estate mogul.

Chapter Seventeen

Her cell phone rang.

Marley didn't have to look at the screen to know who it was. Tony had been calling her almost nonstop the past day and a half.

Well, *nonstop* might have been an exaggeration. However, he had called more often than usual, as if sensing her failure in getting Daniela to accept the Food Network deal.

She hadn't told him yet, and she wasn't looking forward to it.

She winced as her phone trilled the Mission: Impossible theme that was his ringtone. The longer she delayed the inevitable, the angrier he'd be, so she bit the bullet and answered. "Hi, Tony."

"What's this business with Daniela buying a soup kitchen?" he asked without preamble.

"Soup kitchen? I have no idea what you're

talking about," she said truthfully. "I thought you were calling about her refusing to do the Food Network show."

"I'm very disappointed, Marley. I expected better results from you."

It hit her right in the middle of her chest. Instantly, she was a four year old again, being scolded for spilling her milk, or forgetting to pick up her toys, or one of the other list of things that used to drive her mom crazy.

But she wasn't four years old anymore, she reminded herself. She had a voice, and she knew how to use it. "I've been trying to encourage Daniela to accept the gig, but she's been distracted with the guy she's been seeing—"

"*What?*" Tony roared.

Oh no. Damn it. She squeezed her eyes shut. Why did she blurt that out? She hadn't meant to. She tried to backtrack. "I mean, I don't know that she's seeing anyone. I just assumed since she was going out a lot..."

Marley clamped a hand over her mouth. She wasn't helping the situation.

"She hasn't said anything to me about dating anyone. Only about buying some building to open a soup kitchen."

That was what all the secret calculations and plotting were about. She nodded. Interesting idea. Completely crazy, since Daniela's organizational skills didn't extend beyond the kitchen, but interesting nonetheless.

"Who is he?" Tony barked. "What does he do? Have you had him checked out?"

She winced, thinking about how angry Daniela was going to be when she found out she'd spilled the beans to Tony.

Would it annoy her or please her to have someone quiz her about Brian? It seemed like it'd be nice to have someone care so much that he interrogated her about the guy she was dating. Not that she was *dating* Brian. Not really, anyway.

"Marley," Tony snapped. "You're not listening."

"I didn't realize you were finished talking." She slapped a hand over her mouth, horrified that she let that slip. "Sorry, Tony. I didn't mean that exactly."

"Exactly? What the hell is going on out there? You don't sound like yourself either. Are you dating someone, too?"

He said it like it was inconceivable, so she defiantly said, "Yes, I am."

There was stunned silence—on both ends of the line.

She lifted her chin and doubled down. "Brian Benedict is great. Successful, handsome, and funny. And we have great chemistry."

Since he was Italian, Tony spoke effusively anyway, but right now he sounded especially loud. "You and Daniela move across the country, and you go crazy like co-eds on spring break."

"We haven't made any topless videos." Because some devil prodded her, she added, "Yet."

"This conversation is far from finished, Marley." He hung up.

She gripped her phone so tightly it was a wonder the case didn't crack. Her knees should have been trembling, and she should have been afraid for her job. She should have worried that she's blown her chance with Tony. But she felt...

Angry.

How dare he sound like it was such a stretch for her to date someone? She wasn't completely hideous, and she was nice. When she wanted to be, at least.

Men wanted her. Sometimes.

She could prove it. Eyes narrowed, she made another call.

Brian answered right away. "Marley, is the world ending?"

"Not before we go to see a movie together."

"The world is definitely ending if you're asking me to a movie, but I think we can squeeze it in before it's all over. They're showing *Die Hard* at the Castro. It's a Christmas Classic if there ever was one."

"Great," she agreed savagely.

"You want to catch the early showing, or a later one?"

"Early."

"Excellent. I'll pick you up." He paused. "That's what this is about, isn't it? You want me for my ride?"

She smiled, just a little, his light-heartedness crowding her anger away. "It *is* really sexy."

"Damn. I knew it." He sighed dramatically. "I guess I'll have to deal."

She laughed.

"I love that sound. You should make it more. I'll text you before I head over. Marley?"

"Yes?"

"I'm glad you called," he said softly before he hung up.

She set her phone down. She was too.

It was the best moving watching experience *ever*.

Every time Bruce Willis came on the screen, the audience would yell "*McLane!*" They'd boo the bad guys and cheer every time there was an explosion.

But the real magic was with Brian. They shared popcorn with Junior Mints mixed in (her idea) and held hands (his idea).

Marley left the showing high on sugar and happiness. After a sushi snack, they got fresh cookies from next to the theater and cartons of milk and headed to her place.

She still felt fizzy and effervescent when Brian pulled into the driveway and parked—so much so she impulsively said, "Let's have our cookies in the backyard."

"Okay." Brian took her hand and let her lead the way.

The half-moon was their only light, so she went slowly. "I don't come back here that often."

Sweet on You

"It's a shame. It's awesome." Brian nodded at the stone wall fencing the yard in. "Let's sit up there."

"Let's."

She watched him find a toe-hold and boost himself up, following his example less gracefully. She shifted her butt off a sharp spot, letting her legs dangle over the other side.

"Here." He handed her a carton of milk. "Chocolate chip cookie first?"

"Yes." She set the milk next to her and took the half cookie he held out. It was still warm from the oven, the chocolate chips melty and slightly bitter.

"I love cookies like this," Brian admitted. "My best friend's mom used to make cookies like this for us."

"Not your mom?"

"Hell no." He faked a shudder. "My mom is fantastic and talented in many ways that exclude cooking. She manages to burn water."

Marley smiled. "My mom's the same way. Growing up, I knew all the phone numbers for restaurants that delivered by heart."

"But now you have all the warm chocolate chip cookies you want."

She shook her head. "Daniela doesn't bake just for us. These days, she's not around that often either, though she has been baking more."

"Bummer." He held out another cookie. "Snickerdoodle?"

She broke half, swinging her feet, happy. "I didn't know you'd be able to see the lights of Golden Gate Bridge from here."

He nudged her shoulder with his. "Stick with me, kid. I'll take you places."

The brush of his body, even with all the layers of clothing, made her shiver. Impulsively, she turned her head and kissed his cheek.

"You missed." He pointed to his mouth.

Eyes narrowing, she braced herself on the wall, leaned, and kissed him on his lips.

He let her. Literally—he didn't make a move to help or encourage, nothing more than shifting closer to make it easier on her.

Giddy with power, she leaned into him, pressing herself to the side of his body. He tasted sweet, like cinnamon and chocolate. Daniela would have said those were the ingredients for seduction.

Was she ready to seduce?

Confused, she pulled back.

She'd have expected Brian to let her go. He surprised her by catching her by the back of her head. He held her close and took her mouth all over again.

He tore her world apart.

One touch of his lips redefined a kiss in her mind. It was more than the sweet kisses they'd shared before. It whispered of passion and dark need, of perilous heights and thrilling falls. It engulfed and enflamed. It made her soar and grounded her at once.

Something inside her body shifted, melted, came to life. She gasped, holding his arms to keep steady. "I think I just discovered your superpower," she murmured against his talented lips.

"As long as it's your Kryptonite." As he kissed her again, his hand snuck inside her sweater, and she felt it warm and exciting on her skin.

Then he lifted his head, brushing her tingling lips with his thumb, looking into her eyes like all the secrets of life were there. "Go out with me," he said. "On a real date, where it's purposeful, and I bring you flowers and take you to dinner and get nervous about whether you'll let me get to second base after."

"What's this?" Her voice was so husky with desire she didn't recognize it.

"This is an accidental encounter brought on by unseen forces." He held her chin with his fingers. "I'd like to go out once knowing that we're on the same page. That you admit you like me."

"I always liked you."

"Enough to go on a date with me?"

She tried to think of Tony, but the only face in her mind was Brian's. A date with him? That'd be...

Nice.

Fun.

Hot, if making out tonight was any indication.

Maybe Valentine was right. Maybe she should just try it.

So she nodded. "Okay."

"Okay." He exhaled, letting her go. "Good."

Trying not to feel bereft by the loss of touch, she straightened her clothing. "Brian?"

"Marley?" He hopped down from the wall and held his arms open.

She jumped into them, knowing without a doubt that he'd catch her. She slid down his body and braced her hands on his shoulders. "You don't need to worry about getting to second base."

His smile was like the sun rising. "Good to know."

She gave him what she hoped was a mysterious smile and led him back through the garden.

Chapter Eighteen

Daniela slipped into sassy red heels that were going to kill her feet in an hour. But Nico would love them, and he was taking her to the opera tonight, so she figured he deserved some sort of reward.

He hated opera. He hadn't said as much, but she could tell it wasn't his thing. She'd grown up with it. Of course, her brother had grown up with it too, and he hated it, so maybe it was a guy thing.

Nico didn't talk about his childhood—ever. But if she had to guess, she'd have said knife fights in alleyways were the evening entertainments he enjoyed, not opera.

She went downstairs, swinging her purse. Whatever his childhood, he'd made the most of himself. He was successful, determined, and caring, though he'd deny that.

She liked him.

It was sweet now, but she wasn't sure how long it'd last. She couldn't tell how he felt about the fact that she was buying the building. Since the day Chris Ludlow had consented to sell her the building, they'd had a tacit agreement not to discuss it. Would his male ego get over her winning? She wouldn't be sure until she signed the paperwork and it was hers. He said he hated to lose—did he like her enough to overcome that?

Tonight wasn't the night to think about that. One day at a time, she told herself as she reached the first floor.

"Hello, Daniela."

She shrieked, whirling to find her brother sitting in the front room. His tie was loosened and the first couple buttons of his shirt were undone. His feet rested on a table in front of him, and he held a tumbler with whiskey in his hand. He'd turned on the fireplace next to him.

"Tony?" She walked slowly into the room, not believing her eyes. "What are you doing here?"

He smiled but it held no amusement. "Not happy to see me?"

"Actually, no, I'm not." She put her hands on her

hips. "Did Marley know you were coming out?"

"No."

"So…" She shook her head. "Why are you here?"

"Someone has to stop this spring break episode you and Marley have going."

She glanced at the glass in his hand. "How much have you been drinking?"

"I've been wondering the same about you."

"Oh, no, you don't." Pointing a finger at him, she shook her head. "You aren't allowed to come into my house and talk to me like I'm a five year old who can't take care of herself."

"I can when you've been acting like a child." He swirled the ice in the glass. "And this is my house, actually. I'm renting it for you."

Tossing her hair over her shoulder, she glared at him. "Next you'll tell me you're cutting me off from my own money."

"If that's what it takes to get you back on track."

She gasped. "You bastard."

Exhaling, he rubbed his eyes, as though he were exhausted. "Daniela, don't act like I'm the bad guy here. I just want what's best for you."

"You have no idea what's best for me."

"I know that a soup kitchen isn't it." He crossed his arms. "Ever since you moved to San Francisco, you've run unchecked. I've come here to get you back on path."

"I think I can manage my life without your help."

"That's not the impression I get. As far as I can tell, you're determined to destroy everything we've worked so hard to build."

"I didn't realize you were in the kitchen, slaving over the hot oven with me."

"That's not the point, Daniela, and you know it."

His tone was harsh and hurt. She blinked back sudden tears, trying not to remember how he used to call her Dani. She cleared the nostalgia from her throat. "What *is* the point?"

"You have to accept the Food Network deal." He leaned forward, every bit the aggressive businessman his clients paid a fortune for. "It's unprecedented. It'll make you set for life. Then if you want to fritter your life away—"

"I'm frittering my life away *now*," she cried.

"Stop being so melodramatic." He set the glass down and reached for the briefcase next to him. "I brought the paperwork for the network—"

She crossed her arms. "I'm not signing anything."

"As your representative—"

"You're fired."

That stopped him cold. Then he shook his head and spoke to her in that paternal tone that made her want to throw something at his head. "Stop acting like a child, Daniela."

"I'm not acting like anything. I'm dead serious. I don't want you to represent me anymore."

"Who are you going to get then?" he asked, his voice rising.

"No one. I don't want to be a TV star. I just love to bake."

"Are you going through an early midlife crisis?"

She narrowed her eyes. "If you ask me if I'm PMS'ing, I'll throw something at you. Something heavy. Like the bookend you got me for Christmas last year. Or maybe the ugly vase my birthday flowers came in. Remember that one?"

He shook his head. "I have no idea what you're talking about."

"No kidding, because you didn't even order the flowers yourself," she yelled. "Somewhere along the way you stopped being my brother and just became management. Well, I'm done with management. I'd like my brother back."

"Daniela, you're being nonsensical."

"Antonio, you're being an idiot." With one last glare at him, she stormed out.

She heard his heavy footsteps come after her. "Where are you going?" he demanded.

"Out."

"Are you going through some sort of belated rebellious period? Because you hiding things is growing old."

"I'm not hiding anything," she lied, thinking of Nico.

"What about the man you're seeing? Assuming that's why you're going out dressed like that."

Whirling around, she glared at him with her hands on her hips. How had he known? Was Marley spying on her? "Be careful."

He glared right back. "You're the one who needs to be careful. You look like—"

"Like what?"

"Like a harlot."

She burst out laughing. "*Harlot*? Have you been reading Chaucer?"

"I'm glad you think it's funny." Anger made his features harsh. "You know Nonna is probably turning over in her grave over how you look."

"Nonna would be the first one to cheer me on." She would too. She'd have said *Brava, Daniela!* and told her to feed Nico *tiramisu*. Nonna thought *tiramisu* was a great aphrodisiac. "I know exactly what's going on here, and it's not going to work, so knock it off."

"Who's the guy?" her brother persisted.

"None of your business." She lifted her chin.

"It's absolutely my business. I'm your brother."

Daniela snorted.

"What does *that* mean?"

"If you don't know, why don't you have your secretary clue you in? Or maybe Marley, since you're using her as your mole these days." She strode to the door, yanked it open, and walked outside.

She was still flushed and fuming when her cab pulled up to the opera house. Not even seeing Nico leaning against the façade in front cooled her ire.

In fact, seeing him in his tux had the opposite effect on her, rising her temperature up even more. He looked dashing—the suit fit him perfectly—but there was still that air of danger that turned her on.

Sights set on him, she strutted up the steps, grabbed him by the lapel, and kissed him hard.

His hands gripped the back of her dress, holding her to him. When she lifted her head, he said, "Am I being punished for something? If I am, tell me what I did so I can do it again."

She wiped her lipstick from his lips. "You haven't been bad yet, but I'm hoping later."

"Then I can't wait for the opera," he murmured, hand on her back as he escorted her inside.

Daniela lay sweating, face down on Nico's bed, her feet dangling over the edge. The only things she still had on were those uncomfortable heels.

But they were *so* worth the pain. She smiled tiredly against the silky sheets.

Nico rolled onto his side, against her. He pushed her hair aside and kissed the nape of her neck. "You want to tell me what had you so angry earlier. I don't think it was me this time."

"Amazing, isn't it?" She sighed and turned to

face him. "My brother Antonio decided to make a surprise visit."

"How long since you've seen him?"

"Three months."

"But you aren't happy."

"He's come here to manage me." She turned onto her back and stared at the ceiling. "He thinks I'm out of control."

"Are you?"

"Only around you," she joked. Then she sobered. "But maybe I'm supposed to be a little out of control. For the first time in forever, I feel like I'm being myself. Tony doesn't know who that is, and he doesn't care to find out."

"I like you the way you are." Nico nuzzled her.

She smiled and turned into him. "I like me that way too."

"Control is an illusion," he said. "Once you realize chaos is what runs the world, you can use it to your benefit."

"My grandmother always said love runs the world."

His face set into a grim mask. "Love doesn't cause catastrophes and death."

"No, those are just parts of living." She cupped his face. "Love dictates how we react to them though."

He stared at her. She wondered what he was thinking. She wondered what *she* thought—if she wanted him to love her.

The thought caused a hitch of excitement in her chest. "Can I stay tonight?" she asked impetuously.

"Are you sure?"

She could tell he was thinking how she never stayed. But she didn't want to go home and face Tony—not when she felt so happy and hopeful for the future. She wanted to stay and revel in it. "I'm positive," she said.

He gathered her closer. "I'd love you to stay."

"Good." She kissed his shoulder, hopeful. The building was hers—maybe Nico would be, too.

Chapter Nineteen

First base achieved, Brian ran his hand under her coat and top and worked on stealing second.

Marley hummed and arched herself into his touch. "I've never made out on the front stoop of my home before."

"Good," he said, kissing a spot he'd bared on her neck.

"We should do it more often."

"If I knew a nice dinner and oozing chocolate cake was all it took to soften you up, I'd have tried it a long time ago." He lifted his head and resumed kissing her.

She'd never been kissed like this before, like she was the center of his universe and nothing else existed. His hand trailed up her midriff to rest over her breast, fingers trailing delicious circles around the tip.

She loved second base—so much that she wondered about third. She even had a fleeting thought toward a home run, but she knew she wasn't ready to go all the way.

Her breath hitched as his fingers rubbed over the lace of her bra, and she felt a rush of warmth pooling in her center. She twined her fingers in his hair, holding him close, and pressed herself against him.

He luxuriously ended the kiss, whispering against her lips, "I should head home."

"Come inside."

He looked as surprised as she felt. But he recovered almost instantly with, "If I go inside with you, there won't be any funny business."

"Funny business?" she repeated.

"You better keep your hands to yourself." He stepped back and crossed his arms as though protecting himself. "I know your type. You'll get me alone, in your lair, and then grope me. I'm more than a plaything though. I've got feelings and emotions."

"Both feelings and emotions, huh?" she said, tugging her clothes back into place. Her lips felt swollen, and her belly throbbed with distracting need.

"Yeah. So be gentle with me."

"I'll try." She unlocked the door and held it open.

"Are you going to brave it, or do you want to stay outside?"

"Step aside, lady." He entered, craning his neck to look around. Then he lowered his voice. "Take me through the hallowed grounds."

Shaking her head, she took his hand and led him down the hall.

She never knew that holding someone's hand could be such a pleasure. For an accountant, Brian had strong hands, not pale and limp like she'd expect. She liked his hands touching her.

Of course, so far all those touches had been PG. She wondered what a little R-rated action would feel like.

She cleared her throat. "My Batcave consists, basically, of my bedroom, a sitting room, an office, and another large room I use for the rest of my stuff."

"Your *Batcave*?"

"Wait till you see the Justice League." She led him past her bedroom toward her office.

"What's in here?" He stopped in the doorway of her studio and looked in. Before she could stop him, he flipped the light switch.

She wasn't in the habit of sharing her photography with people. Occasionally she gave friends photos she took, like the one she gave Valentine. She'd taken a fair number of them for Daniela over the years as well.

But she'd never had anyone go from frame to frame, judging.

"You took these," Brian said, a note of wonder in his voice. He walked around the room, studying the pictures on the walls before turning his attention to the prints all over the large table in the middle of the room.

She hovered nervously in the doorway, watching him pick up a photo and stare at it before setting it down and going on to the next one.

"You're biting your lip," he commented.

She stopped. Then she frowned. "How would you know? You aren't looking at me."

He glanced up with a smile. "You always bite your lip when you're agitated. It's like you're trying to stop yourself from saying something."

"Maybe."

He stepped up to her and kissed her gently. "Thank you for showing me your art."

She surprised herself by relaxing. "Am I that obvious?"

"Just to me. These are amazing." He shook his head as he moved to the table. "Really, truly amazing. Why aren't you a professional photographer?"

She flushed with pleasure and embarrassment, a creeping warmth that spread from her heart all the way up to the tip of her ears. "That wouldn't be practical. Most photographers don't make enough money to get by."

"Most don't, but most aren't as good as you." He held out a picture.

"That was a little girl at the park behind the house." She shrugged. "I got lucky with that shot."

"It's more than luck. You have a gift."

She shifted from foot to foot. "Want to see my office?"

Brian smiled kindly at her. "Okay, you're done hearing my praise. But that's not to say I won't tell you how great you are later. Can I have this?"

She looked at the print he had in his hand. It was of the one he'd taken of her, from their day on the Embarcadero. "I guess."

"Thanks." He carefully slipped it into his coat pocket. "You were going to show me your office."

"Yes." She turned the light off and led him to the

next room.

"Holy Mother of God." He stood in the doorway and gaped at the full-length posters lining the walls. Finally he said, reverently, "It's the Justice League."

She grinned, pleased that he recognized what she'd done here. Daniela had looked at all the posters and asked why she wanted cartoon posters all over.

Brian turned to her, took her hand, and got on his knees. "Marry me. You're the perfect woman. Anything from this point forward, like if you paraded around in high-heeled boots and lacy things, would just be gravy. Just marry me."

Someone cleared his throat behind her.

She looked over her shoulder, her jaw dropping when she saw Tony standing in the doorway, glaring at Brian. She stepped back, pulling her hand free. "*Tony.*"

"Who's this?" Brian asked, standing.

"That's a question I should be asking." Tony's voice was low and threatening in a way she'd never heard it. "Marley?"

She frowned. "This is Brian Benedict."

Tony gaze fell on Brian like an anvil—an angry anvil.

Clearing her throat, she stepped in front of Brian to divert Tony's wrath. "What are you doing here, Tony? Does Daniela know you're here?"

"Yes, and she was so thrilled she ran out." He turned his glare onto her. "What the hell is going on? I depended on you to keep everything under control and you're running around as wild as my sister."

His disappointment stabbed her right in the center of her chest. Her mind assured her he was completely off base, but in her heart she felt his disapproval and it was acute.

Behind her, Brian shifted. "Wait a—"

She gave him a quelling look over her shoulder before returning her attention to Tony. "It's after business hours, and I told you I was seeing someone."

"Yes. This is very"—Tony eyed Brian like he was imagining stringing him up—"cute."

Brian touched her back and then brushed her hair aside. "Is this him?"

She didn't pretend to misunderstand him. She swallowed, trying to figure out what to say. Before, if Tony had shown up like this, in her living space, she'd have rejoiced. Now she was just wanted him to leave. He was intruding.

It was confusing. She looked at Brian, not sure what she wanted anymore.

Dropping his hand, Brian gazed at her steadily. "It's a simple yes or no question, Marley."

Only it wasn't. "Yes. But—"

"And he has the right to come into your apartment?" Brian asked.

"*My* apartment," Tony corrected. "I rent this home."

"I see." Brian stepped away from her. He looked at her like he wanted her to do something.

Only she didn't know what to do. She looked at Tony and the way he glared at Brian, and she felt paralyzed. She'd always been so sure she wanted Antonio Rossi, but suddenly she wanted to hold Brian's hand and run off giggling with him.

What was happening to her?

"I'll leave then." Brian stood toe-to-toe with Tony, studying him. Then he shook his head, dropped something on her desk, and walked out.

She looked down. Yesterday's Marley grinned at her, a halo of happiness surrounding her in the photo, mocking the misery that was pooling in her chest now.

"Brian," she called after him, but it came out in the barest whisper.

Tony stared after Brian, as if making sure he actually left the house. "Don't worry, Marley. You can do better."

She stiffened, affronted on Brian Benedict's account, because he was pretty great. But before she could stand up for him, Tony walked away. "Meeting tomorrow morning, at nine o'clock," he said, as if he ruled her world.

She looked around. Maybe he did. She just wasn't sure she wanted him to any longer.

Chapter Twenty

NICO ARRIVED HOME to the scent of sweetness and the sound of laughter, and it all came from the kitchen.

He eased out of his suit coat and took it to hang in the bedroom. He slipped off his tie, taking a deep breath as he loosened the top buttons of his shirt.

It'd been a long day of meetings and stubborn people. Now he was home. He'd pour himself a hefty shot of whiskey and spar with the stubborn person who'd been on his mind all day: Daniela.

That morning she'd asked if she could hang out in his suite, because she still didn't feel like going home. He'd pictured coming home to her waiting for him. He'd liked the image so much he'd called the concierge and asked him to get Daniela a few items she'd need for her stay. Minus underwear, of course.

He heard her laugh again, and then the low rum-ble of a male voice. Frowning, he strode out the bedroom and to the kitchen.

She leaned against a counter, a glass of red wine in her hands. She wore one of his shirts, knotted in the front, and a pair of tight jeans the hotel had acquired for her. No bra, which he'd planned but regretted now. Her feet were bare, her face was lit with pleasure, her cheeks flushed, and her lips rosy and moist looking.

Just the same way she looked after making love.

Jason sat at the counter, looking less like a buttoned-up British gentlemen with his shirt collar undone and his tailored jacket off. He had a glass of wine and a large plate of pasta in front of him and stared at Daniela like he was utterly besotted.

Possessiveness flared through Nico, sharp and rigid. Shoving his hands in his pockets to keep from punching his bastard employee, he entered the kitchen.

"There you are," Daniela exclaimed, beaming at him. Her smile slowly faded as she studied his face. "Is something wrong, Nico?"

He glanced at Jason and then back at her. "I didn't realize we were entertaining tonight."

Jason picked up his wine glass. "I stopped by to drop off some paperwork for you. Imagine my surprise when I found a world-famous chef cloistered away in your suite."

He heard the curiosity and accusation in Jason's voice. "It's none of your damn business who I *cloister* in my apartment."

Daniela made a mocking sound.

Facing her, he glared at her.

She tried to look subdued but the humor was more than evident in her eyes as she sauntered up to him. "Hard day, baby?"

"Yes, damn it."

Rubbing his chest soothingly, she bit her lip, either to keep from laughing or to torture him with her sexiness. "Let me pour you a glass of wine and fetch your slippers."

Jason snorted as he shoveled a forkful of pasta into his mouth.

Shooting a dark look at his interfering minion, he shook his head. "I want whiskey."

"Why don't you sit down and I'll get you some?" She kissed his cheek and winked at Jason as she padded out of the kitchen.

Glaring at his right-hand man, the person who supposedly had his back, Nico joined him at the counter.

The man was seemingly unaffected, eating his food with an enthusiasm his British reserve didn't normally allow him to display. "You're full of surprises, Nico," he said after swallowing a bite. "You didn't tell me you'd hired an in-house chef."

"I haven't."

"The only other conclusion I can draw is that you're shacking up with a woman."

He glared. "You're a bastard sometimes, you know that?"

Dabbing a napkin to his mouth, Jason pushed back from the counter and put his coat back on. "I left the paperwork on the waterfront project in China on your desk. Perhaps when you take a break from playing house, you can look over them."

"Get out, Lethem."

Jason just smirked as he tugged down his cuffs. "Don't bollocks this up, Nico. She's the best thing that's ever happened to you, and that's notwithstanding her scrumptious cake."

Daniela came back into the kitchen, tumbler in

hand, frowning when she saw Jason standing. "Are you leaving?"

"Yes, love. The pasta was divine, thank you again." He chastely kissed her cheek. "I will demand your chocolate cake next time."

She smiled in pleasure. "Come by any time."

"Not if you value your life," Nico threatened, taking the glass from her hand and downing a healthy dose.

Daniela shot him a look. "He doesn't mean it."

"Yes, I do."

Jason took her hand and clasped it in both of his. "Nico and I have an understanding, love."

"Understand that I'm going to break your arm if you don't let her go," he growled.

Jason chuckled and lifted her knuckles to his lips, clearly taunting him. But before he could drag her away from his henchman, Jason released her. "Try not to miss me too terribly tonight," he said as he strutted off.

Waiting until she heard the elevator close, Daniela turned to him, hands on her hips. "What was that about?"

"You tell me." He scowled. "I came home to find

you half naked, flirting with my employee."

She looked down at myself. "What are you talking about? I'm fully dressed."

"You're wearing my shirt without a bra."

"But I'm wearing pants, which is more than I had on an hour before Jason arrived."

Something inside him roared at the idea of another man seeing what was only his. Not wanting to examine that emotion, he picked her up by the waist, hefted her on top of the counter, and leaned his head against her chest.

She stroked his hair. "Poor baby, feeling cranky."

"You're subverting my employees."

"Just one, and he was already a fan." She kissed the top of his head. "Don't worry. I have a thing for the boss."

"Do you?" he murmured, relaxing for the first time all day.

"Apparently I like overbearing men."

He kissed her skin at the open vee of the shirt. "Lucky for me." And he meant it.

Chapter Twenty-one

Daniela held up one of the scones from the Mandarin Oriental's tea service and made a face at it. "It's good, but it's not nearly as good as yours, Eve."

Blushing prettily, Eve tucked her hair behind her ear. "That's sweet of you to say."

"It's true." Lola stretched toward the tower. "But the cucumber cream cheese sandwiches are divine."

"The whole teatime experience is divine." Eve looked around the suite. "We're on top of the world here."

"It was the least I could do to thank you for helping me." She wasn't sure she wanted Marley to report back to Tony on her, so she'd asked Eve and Lola to bring over some of her things. Not that she'd needed a lot—the Mandarin Oriental was amazingly obliging in fetching whatever she'd needed. Except underwear, but she suspected Nico was behind that oversight.

"You haven't told us *why* we're ensconced in the ritziest room in one of the most expensive hotels in the country much less San Francisco, eating little crustless sandwiches and sipping tea." Lola lifted her cup. "We've been patient, but that's only because you had food waiting for us. You'll have anarchy on your hands soon."

Daniela smiled. She *had* been cryptic when she'd called them and invited them over to Nico's suite for tea, but she hadn't wanted to get into it over the phone. "I was restless, so I thought I'd invite my friends over for tea."

"Please excuse me," Lola said, reaching for a truffle, "but, delicately put, that's bullshit. Since when did you start hanging out at the Mandarin Oriental instead of your own mausoleum?"

"Mausoleum?" Eve asked with an amused lift of her eyebrow.

Lola shrugged. "I've got a way with words."

"Right now, the mausoleum is housing my brother, and since he's not my favorite person, I decided to come stay here." She paused. "In Nico's place."

Lola sat up, alert. "Nico? Is that the guy you're seeing? He *lives* here?"

"Is he around?" Eve whispered, craning her neck.

"He's in the study working." She'd interrupted him to tell him she'd invited a couple friends over, and that she was ordering tea if he wanted any. He'd replied that he only wanted her. She smiled wickedly, remembering when he'd shown her how much.

Lola nudged Eve. "Look at the expression on her face. I had that expression when I first started getting it on with Sam."

"You still get that expression when you talk about Sam."

"What can I say? My man is a god in bed."

"So is Nico," Daniela said with a wink.

The women stared at her and then burst into raucous laughter.

"So tell us about him," Eve insisted, pouring more tea for them all. "How long have you been seeing him?"

"Not that long." It seemed like a whirlwind, like she just met him yesterday *and* had known him forever. "But we've been seeing each other—"

"Otherwise known as 'getting it on,'" Lola interjected.

"—pretty regularly." She picked up a shortbread

and dunked it in the earl grey. "So when my brother arrived unannounced, it seemed natural to crash here for the duration."

"Natural?" Lola eyed her in disbelief. "Natural is staying with a girlfriend, or someone's empty apartment. Natural isn't shacking up with a man you just met. Not unless you're really into him."

Daniela shook her head. "It's not like that. I'm just taking a timeout."

"Beauty took a timeout in the beast's castle," Lola pointed out, "and look how that turned out."

"Nico isn't a beast." She pursed her lips in thought. "Usually."

Eve put a hand on her arm. "Daniela, in her own creative way, Lola's trying to say that it seems serious with your guy if you're living with him."

"Can we really call me staying in his suite while my brother lays siege on my house 'living with him?'"

"*Yes*," both her friends said.

She grinned sheepishly. "I guess this is where I confess he cleared out part of his closet so I could hang my clothes."

"What does he do that he lives in a hotel?" Eve asked. "Does he travel a lot?"

"He's in real estate." She shrugged. "He hasn't traveled since we met."

"That means he likes you," Lola declared. "A man would have to be a fool to leave when he just met a woman he liked, without securing her affections or taking her with. If this guy—what's his name?"

"Nico." Saying it was like letting chocolate melt on your tongue.

"If Nico is as successful as this suite suggests, he's no fool." Lola leaned forward, her blue eyes wide with excitement. "The question is, how much do you like him. A lot, if this is your sanctuary."

Eve lifted her teacup to her lips. "You obviously feel comfortable and safe around him."

"I really—"

Just that moment, she heard the door to his office open and then the light sound of his bare feet on the hardwood floors.

They fell silent, all three of them turning toward the hallway right as Nico stepped into the room. He wore jeans with an untucked shirt open at the collar, and his hair was rumpled like he'd run his hands through it in frustration.

He was gorgeous. Daniela wanted to go up to

him and tear his shirt off.

She glanced at Lola and Eve. Her friends gawked at him. She knew they understood what she saw in him.

They turned to her, and then they all burst into laughter.

Nico's brow furrowed as he moved to her side and ran a possessive hand down the length of her hair. "That's not the usual reaction I get when I walk into a room."

Daniela lifted her face. "There's a first time for everything. Nico, these are my friends Eve and Lola."

"Ladies." He smiled at her friends and then dropped a kiss on her lips. "I'll leave so you can continue to discuss me."

Something warmed in the pit of her stomach as she watched him leave, something that didn't have anything to do with carnal pleasure and everything to do with affection. She'd only been here a couple days, but she wasn't ready to go home. Even if Tony went back to New York, she'd stay here.

"You do like him," Eve said softly, a twinkle in her eyes. "You're visually eating him up like he's a chocolate croissant."

She turned to them. "How do you know if you're in love? How did you guys know with your men?"

Lola and Eve both shrugged, but it was Lola who said, "It's different for everyone. But, really, Daniela, the answer's inside you if you're honest with yourself."

She looked inward, wondering. If Nonna were here, she'd tell her to make *zabaglione* and stir in thoughts of him—if it came out sweet, it meant she was in love. If it curdled, he wasn't right for her.

But Lola was right—she didn't need to make *zabaglione* to know. The answer was there in every beat of her heart.

Nico stood in his bathroom. His once-tidy counter was covered in mysterious feminine things. There was enough makeup piled there to stock a department store. When Daniela had said she called her assistant and asked her to deliver "a few things" she'd need while she stayed with him, he hadn't expected this.

Oddly, he hadn't minded either. It was... not bad, actually. The noise and the clutter of having someone else around was actually nice.

He picked up the random fluff of underwear from the floor. Red: his favorite color.

He smiled at it. No, it wasn't bad having Daniela there—at all.

He'd never pictured himself living with anyone, much less someone like Daniela. Jason was right: Nico would never have picked someone like her because she was too messy.

She made him too messy.

The stillness from the other room informed him the women were gone. He tossed the panties in the laundry hamper and walked out into the living room. He stood in the entryway, watching Daniela clean up the detritus from her impromptu tea party. He'd liked seeing her with her friends, even if they'd burst into girlish giggles the moment he'd walked into the room.

It made him wonder what she told them about him.

"If you know what's good for you, you'd help me carry this into the kitchen," she said without turning around.

Grinning, he slipped behind her and gripped her around the waist.

"That's not helping," she murmured.

But he could hear the smile in her voice, and he nuzzled her neck. "It's helping me a lot."

Laughing, she set the things back on the table and turned in his arms. She circled his neck with her arms and kissed him.

It never got old. Every touch, kiss, embrace was new and different. Exciting. "Remind me to give Jason a bonus."

"What?"

"Nothing." He smiled. "Did you have a good time with your friends?"

"Yes." She smiled happily. "I love them. I haven't had female friends since I graduated from high school. Culinary arts are so competitive, and I worked so much, and Tony was my best friend, anyway..."

Her voice trailed off, some of the brightness fading from her expression.

It surprised him how much he didn't like seeing her light dimmed. He touched the corner of her mouth with his thumb. "But now you have me, and those women, who were frightening, by the way."

She laughed, like he meant her to. "How were they frightening?"

"They looked like they were hungry and I was the main course." He pretended to shudder.

Laughing more, she pushed his shoulder. "You loved it. And they didn't look at you that way. They're both happily taken with studs of their own."

"Are you saying I'm a stud?"

"That's what you're always telling me." She smirked at him.

Bending, he put his shoulder into her waist and lifted her over his shoulder.

"Nico!" she shrieked. "Put me down."

"Okay." He took her to the couch, set her on top, and covered her with his body.

Laughing, she pretended to push him away. "You're a brute."

"You love that about me."

"I do." She warmly gazed up at him, running her hand along his jaw.

He kissed her palm. "What do you want to do tonight? I have a couple excellent suggestions."

"Both of which probably exclude clothing."

"No. I'm perfectly happy letting you wear those red shoes."

Grinning, she pulled him down and gave a loud

kiss. "Have I told you how happy I am? Which is incredible, when you consider the season."

"I'd have thought someone like you would love Christmas."

"Someone like me?" she asked with a lift of her eyebrow.

"Full of light. Sweet." He kissed her and, like always, was surprised just how sweet she tasted.

She hummed, licking her lips when he lifted his head. "You're implying that 'someone like you' doesn't like Christmas."

"I don't." He sat up, but he kept his hand on her leg. He couldn't *not* touch her. "Christmas wasn't a great time of year in my household growing up."

She sat up, studying him solemnly. Finally, she said, simply, "I'm sorry for that."

"The past is the past."

"I wish I could have shared my grandmother with you. She did Christmas big." She took his hand, her expression soft. "My first memories are of Christmas. She used to decorate every inch of her house, and I'm not exaggerating. She had lights and holly on everything. She made my Nonni put up so many figures and lights outside their house that he complained it took him a week to finish. Theirs was the house you'd drive by at night to gawk at."

His childhood residence had been one to drive by as well — to drive by and shoot at. "You love your grandmother."

"She was amazing. She's the reason I bake. My first memories are of me sitting on her counter, helping her. By 'helping,' I mean I'd eat the fistful of raw dough she'd give me to play with. She'd play Frank Sinatra and Dean Martin and Bing Crosby in the background, and sometimes she'd pick me up and dance. When I got older, we'd plan all the cookies we're going to make weeks ahead of time, and then we'd spend a week baking from dawn till late at night." Some of the light in her eyes dimmed. "Nonna died last year before Christmas."

He caressed her hair away from her face. "And it's not the same?"

"Not at all." She pursed her lips. "Although, this year is better. I think because I have a purpose with the soup kitchen. And because there's that family squatting in the building."

"I don't understand."

"I realized they probably won't have Christmas.

Maybe they never have." Her brow furrowed at the thought. "It's just awful to think that."

He was torn between wanting to protect her naïveté and instructing her on how the real world worked. "That's life."

"It doesn't have to be." Her face lit up, fiery, like an unbending goddess. "If people just did a little something, things could change."

"Things only change for people who make it happen."

"*I'm* going to change things." She lifted her adorable chin. "I bought them Christmas presents."

He gazed at her steadily, not letting any of his thoughts show on his face. He was both endeared and irritated by her devotion to that homeless family. "It seems like more than enough that you take them food."

"It's not enough."

"It's also not your responsibility."

She frowned at him. "If I don't take responsibility, those kids will starve and freeze to death."

"They're street kids. They know how to take care of themselves."

"They're *kids*." She glared at him, pulling back.

"No kids should have to take care of themselves."

But that wasn't how the world worked. He felt that hardened spot in his chest pulse righteously. Some kids didn't luck out. Some kids ended up dead.

"You don't agree." Daniela's eyes narrowed and she crossed her arms. "You don't give a damn about them."

"They don't have to be where they are."

"They're *kids*," she yelled at him.

"They have a choice."

"Easy for you to say."

It was, because he'd been there. "You aren't going to be able to be their guardian angel forever, you know. You're headed for heartbreak. They're on the street because they don't have it in them to be anywhere else."

She got up to her knees, pointing at him. "You're the Grinch."

"Yes, I am. And I'm a realist, and no number of presents is going to help those kids in their situation."

"Well, I'm not inviting you to help me deliver them."

He narrowed his eyes. "And, yet, I'm still going with you."

She folded her arms and glared. Then she grabbed his shirt and kissed him hard. "You *infuriate* me, but thank you. For going with me," she added softly.

He *melted*, damn it. He didn't know whether to growl or roll over and expose his belly.

Fortunately, her phone rang them. She shifted to pick it up from the table. Making a sour face, she tossed it aside.

He wondered who it was that got such a reaction. "You didn't want to answer it?"

"It was my brother. He's just going to be overbearing."

Maybe because he was already on edge. Maybe because his perspective was different. Maybe because he could understand how frustrating it was to care for her. But he couldn't keep quiet. "Your brother cares about you. You should appreciate that. I'd give anything to have my older brother meddle in my life."

"But he doesn't, because he knows you're capable."

"He doesn't because he's dead."

She gasped, her hand tightening on his as she shifted to face him. "I'm sorry. I didn't know."

He was just as startled by the statement as she was. He'd never told anyone. Nico swallowed the sudden lump in his throat. "He died protecting me," he said, his voice low and raw even to his own ears.

Then she wrapped herself around him and squeezed. "I'm so sorry," she whispered against his neck. "I didn't know."

He squeezed her back, like she was his anchor, grounding him. He shifted her onto his lap and buried his head in the crook of her neck.

"Want to tell me about it?" she asked after a while.

"No." Sighing, he relented. "Our mom was into drugs, and everything else you could imagine, so Eddie took care of me. I don't remember a time when he didn't look out for me. He cooked for me and made me go to school, even though he dropped out in the fifth grade. He told me I had a brain, and that I had street smarts, and with the two I'd be able to do things."

"And you did."

"Eddie made sure of it. He wouldn't let me get distracted. He was so determined that I get out of that shithole that he joined the local gang to make money, to keep a roof over our head and to save for my college fund."

"Oh no," Daniela breathed, holding him tighter.

"He got in over his head. I don't know what they wanted him to do, but he refused, and the next thing I knew, he turned up on our doorstep, shot five times. I found him. It's been over twenty years, and I still remember every detail of that night."

She shook her head, a small sob escaping under her breath. "I didn't know."

Frowning, he lifted her chin. "Are you crying?"

"Of course, I'm crying," she exclaimed. "It's *sad*. I hate my brother right now, because he's a high-handed, selfish bastard, but I'd be devastated if he died. I'm so sad for you I want to go bake you sugar cookies."

Amazingly, he felt the hard spot on his chest loosen, and the beginning of a smile curve his lips. "Will that make me happy?"

"My grandmother always said they would." She sniffled, wiping her eyes on his shirt. Then she kissed his jaw. "If they don't work, there's always me."

"Yes, there is." He kissed her, gently, wholly, the way she deserved to be kissed. "It's working already."

Chapter Twenty-two

MARLEY STOOD OUTSIDE of Valentine's subterranean office, her hand on the door handle. She should just go in. She started to open the door.

No, she shouldn't. She stopped, biting her lip. Maybe getting Brian's address wasn't a great idea.

Except she *missed* him. She'd been sitting in her office, surrounded by the mildly disappointed faces of the Justice League, trying to work on the list Tony had given her in his effort to "set Marley and his sister right."

She rolled her eyes. So far, the only thing he'd managed was to drive Daniela out of the house. They hadn't heard from her in days. She wasn't even returning Marley's calls.

That made Marley feel bad, like she let down someone who was supposed to count on her no matter what. She wanted to talk to Brian about it, but he wouldn't answer her calls either.

Which made her feel doubly bad. She'd lost the only two friends she had.

The days since she'd last seen Brian were awful. They'd dragged on forever, gray and dull, without anything to look forward to. She'd have given anything to hang out with him — to see a movie or dangle their feet over the stone wall as they shared cookies.

She missed kissing him.

She sighed. She *really* missed kissing him.

So she pressed on the handle and went inside.

Sitting primly on one of the gilded chairs, Valentine set her phone down. "I wondered if you were going to come in or not."

"I wasn't sure it was a good idea." She sat down, unwinding the lime green scarf. "I didn't know if you'd be angry with me."

Valentine regarded her silently, then shrugged. "I'm a matchmaker, so I've seen it all. But Brian's a friend of mine, so I'm disappointed for him. He liked you."

Liked. She winced at the past tense. "You've talked to him?"

"Not much."

But enough to be annoyed with her — Marley got that much from Valentine's body language. "I need to see him, but he won't answer my calls. I don't suppose you'd give me his address, would you?"

"I'm not sure that's a good idea."

The thought of not talking to Brian sent her over the edge. She leaned forward, intent on making Valentine understand. "I just want to talk to him. He and I have become friends in the past weeks and I feel bad leaving things the way they stand."

"That's all?" Valentine asked mildly. "You just want to fix your friendship?"

"No. Yes." She threw her hands in the air and fell back against the seat back. "I don't know. I thought we were friends."

"I thought you loved someone else."

She shook her head. "I don't know how I feel about anything. When I start to think about it, my head just hurts."

"You need to figure it out."

"I thought I had it figured out," she wailed. "I thought I loved Tony, but he's been around the house for days and instead of being excited I've just been annoyed. I try to avoid him at all costs. I even ducked into a closet to hide from him when he was calling for me."

"If you want my professional opinion, that's a bad sign."

She ignored her friend's sarcasm. "I thought if I talked to Brian, it might make it all clear somehow."

Valentine said nothing, watching her like impassively as though she were a psychiatrist.

Marley took a deep breath. "I just want to talk to him. Please, Valentine."

"I'll give you his address on one condition."

"What is it?"

"You have to kiss him." Valentine crossed her arms, looking like a militant cupid. She leaned forward, eyes blazing. "And not just a peck on the cheek. You have to kiss him with all the passion in your soul. That's the only way you're going to know."

Kissing Brian had never been the problem, so she nodded. "Okay."

Valentine picked up her phone and tapped the screen. "I texted it to you. Go now. I know he's home."

"Thank you." Getting up, she impulsively hugged her and then ran out the door.

By the time she flagged a cab and made it to

Brian's apartment, she'd started to get cold feet. She stood on his doorstep, just like she had on Valentine's, not sure what to do.

He took the decision out of her hands by opening the door. "I can hear you creaking on the porch."

"Oh." She tried to smile but she was afraid she only managed a sickening grimace. "Hi."

He arched his brow. "That's all you've got for me?"

"No. Can I come in?"

Straightening his glasses, he stepped aside.

She gave his apartment a quick look, surprised that it was so tidy considering he didn't know she was coming over. Then she gasped, seeing the framed artwork on the walls. There was an entire series, all superheroes, ending with a simple abstract painting of Catwoman. "You have superheroes too," she said, dumbfounded.

"I doubt that's why you came over," he said, leaning against a wall.

"No, it's not." But it struck her hard for some reason. She tried to clear her head and focus on why she was there. "I had things I wanted to say, but I can't quite put them into words."

"Then how about I get some things off my chest?"

That didn't seem like a good idea, but she was so off-balanced she found herself saying, "Okay."

"When I said before that I wasn't interested in dating you, I was lying." He shrugged. "I'd hoped the reverse psychology would work on you. I shouldn't have tried. Hell, I shouldn't even be interested. Your priorities are screwed up. I don't need that."

She didn't know what to address first, so she just focused on the last part. "My priorities are fine."

"You're wasting your life working as a slave for someone just because you like her brother. Can you argue that?"

She clamped her mouth shut.

"See?" he said gently. "And the thing is, what are you wasting it for? Nothing, because that guy is never going to return your affections."

"I—"

"He doesn't even see you," Brian continued. "You're so far off his radar, it's not even funny. I don't even know that you really like him. He's just a substitute for the father you never had. Any idiot could see that."

Tony, the father she never had? The idea was

preposterous—and kind of true. But she wasn't going to think on that now. She had to focus on what was important here. "I didn't come to talk about Tony. I came to talk about you."

Brian stuck his hands in his pockets. "There's nothing to talk about. You made your feelings clear."

"No, I haven't. I've barely gotten a word in edgewise."

"So what do you want, Marley? Because it seems to me you don't know. Or, at the very least, what you want isn't what I was offering."

"What were you offering?" she asked, her voice barely a whisper.

"A friend and partner in crime. Someone who understands you, who likes you even when you're not at your best." He got in her face. "I wanted *you*, not some ideal that existed only in my head but the true package. All funny, snarky, quirky parts of it."

"You wanted?" She swallowed. "Past tense?"

"I'd be a fool to chase someone who doesn't want me to catch her, wouldn't I?"

That was the thing. Maybe she did want him to catch her. She thought about the way she felt when he kissed her, the tingly excitement. She thought about how happy she felt after she'd been with him. She'd never felt that way with anyone.

But she was scared. What if she told Brian all that she he walked away? He was already halfway out the metaphorical door.

Maybe she *was* really screwed up.

"I'll go," she said softly, bowing her head.

She wanted him to stop her. She wanted him to take her in his arms and convince her to stay. But he opened the door for her to leave.

She did, and it wasn't until much later she realized she hadn't been able to keep her promise to Valentine. She hadn't kissed Brian, and she was pretty sure she'd never get the chance to.

Chapter Twenty-three

"Give me good news," Daniela said into the phone when she answered her real estate agent's call.

"We lost the building."

"Where did it go?" she asked as she walked into the kitchen.

"No, we were outbid," Ken explained patiently. "Cruz Enterprises bought it."

"That's not possible." She stopped abruptly in the middle of the kitchen. "I made an agreement with Chris Ludlow. I took him three loaves of cinnamon bread."

"Well, it must not have made the same impression Cruz's offer did."

"How much was his offer?"

"Half a mill over what we bid."

She sat down, on the floor, abruptly.

"Daniela? Are you still there?"

"Barely," she said, staring unseeingly ahead. "Is there anything we can do?"

"About this property? No. Cruz closed on it. But I can look again for other buildings that might work, within your budget. Maybe we'll have better luck after the holidays."

"I'll let you know. Thank you, Ken."

"I'm sorry, Daniela. I wish I could do more."

"It's not your fault." It was Nico's.

She hung up but stayed on the floor, staring at the cupboards in front of her. She'd been staying with him for days. *Days*. When had he made the deal? When had he signed the papers?

She should have been upset because he got the building, but, damn him, she was more upset because he hadn't been honest with her. Why had he hid the fact that he'd outbid her? To surprise her one night when they were soaking in his Jacuzzi tub? Did he think she wouldn't find out?

Anger boiled in her chest, like a pot of Nonna's *penne a la arrabiata*.

She'd make some now, she decided. She got up, determined, needing to channel her fury into something.

Nico ordered food in all the time, but after she'd decided to stay she'd stocked up on some essentials so she could cook. Nonna's *arrabiata* sauce was simple to make, needing only tomatoes, passion, and time.

She had plenty of the last two ingredients, thanks to Nico. That *bastard*.

Determined, grim, she strode to the wine rack and looked through all the bottles first. She stopped when she saw the '82 Chateau Margaux.

"Why not?" She plucked it out and uncorked it. Pouring herself a large glass, she sipped it, nodded in approval, and set a pan on the burner for her sauce.

She was on her second glass, about to toss the cooked pasta into the spicy tomato sauce when she heard the elevator doors open. She picked up the wine bottle, looking at it regretfully. A waste, but it was going to feel so satisfying.

"Daniela?" Nico walked into the kitchen.

She threw the bottle at his head.

He ducked just in time. The bottle hit the wall behind him and broke, making a splatter pattern of wine over the white walls and carpets.

Nico swiped what splashed on his cheek and tasted it. "Good vintage."

"When were you going to tell me?"

He looked resigned. "I told you all along that I was going to buy the property. It shouldn't have been a surprise."

She downed the wine in her glass and threw that at him, too. "Bastard."

He ducked again. "Daniela, you're going to run out of things to throw at me. Let's just stop and discuss this."

"We could have discussed this," she yelled, "if you'd told me. *But you didn't.*"

Holding his hands out to try to calm her down, he approached her cautiously. "It's just a building. I'll help you find another one that suits your purposes. I know there's that family living in it. I won't turn them out without a care. I'll find a place for them too."

"*That's not the point*. The point is you didn't tell me. I'm living here with you, and you didn't mention a word to me. How do you think that makes me feel?"

Of all the things he could have said, she didn't expect him to go with "I needed to buy that building, Daniela."

"Well, you got what you needed." Wiping her hands on a towel, she tossed it on the counter and walked toward the bedroom.

"Where are you going?" he said, following her.

"Home," she said, not bothering to turn around.

He caught up to her and made her turn. "Daniela, you have to understand—"

"Do you know what I understand?" She got in his face, wanting to kiss it as much as she wanted to spit at it. "I understand that I told you my dream, what I wanted so badly, and you disregarded it. More than that, you went ahead with your own plans, even though they directly conflicted with mine. But most of all, you kept me in the dark. How is that different than Tony? You should have had my back, but you stabbed it instead."

"You're being dramatic," he said.

"And you're being an asshole."

He tugged her against him and kissed her. There was the residual taste of sweetness and spice, but the overtone of bitterness overwhelmed everything else.

She broke away from him, putting a hand to her mouth. Her lips felt bruised, but not nearly as much as her heart. "You screwed up," she said in a low voice. And then she turned and walked straight to the elevator.

She realized she didn't have shoes on when she got to the lobby, but she didn't care. She had the porter flag her a taxi, and she numbly rode home, calling Marley to ask her to come pay for the cab once she realized she didn't have her purse.

Marley was waiting out by the curb when she pulled up. Looking as grim as Daniela felt, she paid the driver and then studied Daniela head to toe. "You look like I feel," she finally said. "Man problems?"

"What else could it be? You?"

Marley sighed so hardily Daniela almost smiled. She slung her arm through her assistant's and walked gingerly into the house.

Tony was inside, waiting. Fuming. "Where the hell have you been, Daniela?"

"Put a sock in it, Antonio."

"Fine!" He threw his arms in the air. As he stormed out, he yelled, "Ruin your lives. You'll come running back to me soon enough."

"As if." Daniela turned to Marley. "You and I are getting a bottle of wine, some chocolate, and retiring to my room."

"Kinky," Marley said.

Daniela smiled in shock. "Marley, that was funny."

She rolled her eyes. "You want funny? I have a story to tell you about the wrong man who got away."

"Will one bottle of wine be enough?" she asked, an arm through Marley's as they headed to the kitchen.

"Probably not, because I may have to quit tonight too."

"Damn." Daniela looked at her assistant. "Are you really giving notice?"

Marley took a deep breath and nodded. "Yes," she said, sounding sure. "Yes, I am. I'm going to focus on my photography."

"Good for you." Daniela hugged her tightly.

After a moment, the younger woman returned the embrace. "You aren't angry?"

"What I am is impressed. It takes courage to step out on your own." She went straight to the fridge and pulled out champagne and truffles. "I know you don't drink, but you're making an exception tonight. We're going to toast your new endeavor, curse our men, and generally get trashed."

"I'll get the glasses," Marley offered helpfully.

Chapter Twenty-four

It started out simple: Daniela invited Eve and Lola. But Eve brought Olivia, and Lola brought Gwen, and suddenly it was a party—on the floor of Daniela's unfinished showroom space.

Lola ran back to her apartment and brought a blanket, and Olivia contributed candles from her shop since Daniela still didn't have the lighting wired. Eve brought over champagne, and Gwen brought her happy laugh.

They sat on the floor, with a couple jackets piled around Olivia to help her get comfortable. Daniela eyed the woman's belly with awe and a little envy. Olivia was very pregnant—radiant the way women aspired to be. "Are you comfortable, Olivia?"

"I'm perfect." She smiled as she stretched her legs in front of her. "Although I'll be more comfortable when Sprout decides to make his appearance."

"I hope he decides to make his appearance after tonight," Lola said, handing over a glass of sparkling grape juice to Olivia. "Because I don't know how to birth babies, Miss Scarlet."

Grinning, Eve passed around champagne to the rest of them. "Maybe we should toast to long-term projects finally coming to fruition."

"Are you trying to tell me something?" Daniela looked around her pathetic showroom.

"When are you going to finish it?" Gwen asked. "I haven't seen anyone working in here for weeks."

"I'm having second thoughts."

Eve set down her glass abruptly. "You aren't leaving San Francisco, are you?"

"No." She shook her head vehemently. "I love it here. What I'm reconsidering is continuing baking."

"What would you do?" Eve asked.

She shook her head, not wanting to talk about her soup kitchen idea. Maybe it was as ridiculous as Tony said. "I had some ideas, but I have no idea. Sometimes things don't turn out the way you want."

"Uh-oh." Lola reached for a brownie. "This feels like a story involving a man."

"There is no man." She reached for a cookie and

savagely bit into it, imagining it was Nico's head.

Gwen laughed. "You aren't fooling anyone here. You might as well give us the details."

"You'll feel better," Olivia said, accepting the cookie Eve handed her. "It'll get it out of your system faster."

"Which means you'll forgive him faster, and then you can get on to the make up sex." Lola winked at her.

"I'm not going to forgive him," she declared, downing her champagne and holding out her glass for more. "Nico Cruz is dead to me."

"You're so Italian sometimes." Eve refilled her glass. "But you obviously really like him, so at some point you have to be less Italian and forgive him a little."

"But it's totally okay to make his life hell first," Lola added.

"I threw a wine bottle at his head." She smiled grimly, still feeling the satisfaction of it. "An '82 Chateau Margaux."

Eve choked on her drink, and Gwen launched into raucous laughter. Lola looked at them, her brow furrowed. "I guess that's an expensive bottle of wine?"

"It's only like a couple thousand a bottle," Gwen said, wiping her eyes.

Daniela forgot that Gwen was heiress to one of France's most prestigious wineries. Gwen was always so unassuming, in her hippie chick clothing. But of course she'd know her wine.

"It was probably sacrilege to waste it like that, but it made me happy," Daniela said, reaching for a biscotti. "I had a glass before I threw it at him. It was delicious."

"What did he do that was so unconscionable?" Olivia asked.

She started to say that he stole the building that she wanted out from under her, only that wasn't what had her most angry. She didn't understand why he needed to buy it so badly, but the reason didn't matter. What upset her was that he hadn't been honest with her. The entire time they'd been together, he'd hid what he was doing, and that was what hurt. "He went behind my back."

Her friends didn't say anything, obviously waiting for more.

She shrugged. "I got angry because he didn't trust me enough to tell me what he was doing. I found out through a second party."

"And it chaffed, finding out from someone else." Lola nodded. "Classic conflict."

"The question now is, when are you going to forgive him?" Olivia said, popping another sweet in her mouth.

"Never," Daniela declared ruthlessly, even though her heart wilted a little at that prospect.

"Is that in your best interests?"

"I'd be happy if I never saw him again," she said viciously.

"Liar," Lola said with a smile. "If you didn't care about him, you wouldn't be so worked up."

Gwen leaned forward and fake-whispered, "You may even be in love with him."

"I *refuse* to love him." She set her glass down before she was tempted to throw it. "Especially an overbearing, macho man who pats me on the head and dismisses me instead of sharing important things with me."

"He's kind of like your brother, then," Eve stated.

They all looked at the blonde.

Eve shrugged. "She's told me about him, and he's been coming into the shop. I guess Marley must have told him we're friends, because he's been asking me about you."

"That bastard." If Tony were here, she wouldn't resist throwing her glass at him.

"He's confident to say the least, but he seems like he wants the best for you," Eve said. "He seemed worried, and it wasn't pretend-worry."

"Tony doesn't bother pretending." Daniela frowned. "He really asked about me?"

"Yes. I don't know him normally, but he seemed tired and worn out. And sad." Eve looked at him. "He said it's the first year your family isn't having Christmas together."

"Nonna used to host it. Now that she's gone and our parents are traveling, it's just the two of us. It hardly seems worth it." But it made her sad, nonetheless.

"There's something to be said for family," Gwen said, "even if they suck. Fortunately, not all family is biological."

"Hear, hear to that." Lola lifted her glass in a toast. "To new family and girl time, both of which are sacred."

"Happy holidays, ladies." Olivia raised her glass,

too. "May you get your heart's desire."

"And lots of good loot," Lola added.

They all looked at her.

"What?" She took a cookie. "I may write romance, but I can be a realist sometimes."

Chapter Twenty-five

"You made a mess of it, didn't you?"

Nico glanced up from the contract he wasn't really reading because he couldn't focus on the words. "Excuse me?"

Jason gave him an arch, British look that conveyed disappointment on a cellular level. "I saw that you won the bid on the Harrison building."

He returned his employee's look with a hard one of his own. "I told you I intended to make that purchase."

"Yes, but that was before Daniela."

Shoving the documents aside, he whirled in his chair and stared unseeing out the window.

Jason cleared his throat. "You know I don't infringe on your privacy—"

Nico snorted.

"—but as your right hand, I feel I need to speak

up this time, because you're making the biggest mistake of your life."

It certainly felt that way, but he'd made a promise to his brother. He clenched his jaw. Eddie gave his life for him—this was the least he could do.

Unaware of his inner dialogue, Jason continued in his clipped voice. "Is this property so important that you're willing to destroy the best thing that's ever happened to you?"

"I need air." The chair skittered as he stood. He blew by Jason and grabbed his coat off the hook. "Look over those contracts for me."

"Think about what you're doing while you're out," Jason called after him. "And don't come back until you've made the right decision."

Nico left the building, barely noticing the greetings the guards called out to him. He walked down California Street. He stopped at a liquor store and bought a bottle of Jim Beam before continuing on to the Embarcadero, past the Ferry Building, and right on Harrison.

His steps slowed as he neared the building.

It was nothing like the night he'd found Eddie on the sidewalk. That night had been still, with a full moon illuminating the night's evilness. Tonight, there wasn't a sliver of moonlight to be had, but it didn't lessen his uneasiness. He tensed as he strode up the walkway.

Nico sat on the front stoop of his newly acquired building, the bottle of Jim Beam in his hands. He took a slug of the whiskey, grimacing. He held the bottle out to pour it on the sidewalk when a stiff breeze all but knocked him upside the head.

It'd just been the wind — logically he knew that — but for some reason he had the feeling Eddie was lurking somewhere in the periphery, smirking at him. *Little bro, sometimes I think you ain't got any brains in that big head of yours*, he'd have said.

"I know," Nico muttered, shaking the rest of the liquor out of the bottle. Because he suspected trading in Daniela's love for this decrepit building was a colossal mistake.

Not that Daniela had said the words to him. He wasn't a connoisseur of love, or anything about it, but there was something more than just lust between the two of them.

He missed her.

All day he sniffed the air, searching for the scent

of her baking. He didn't trip on random articles of clothing, or find underwear in odd corners of his apartment. In the mornings, he woke up reaching for her.

It was a gnawing ache, deep in his gut.

Something rustled close to him, and he turned, knowing instinctively it wasn't the wind.

A little girl stood eight feet away, staring at him with the biggest eyes he'd ever seen.

He didn't know what to say, so he fell on an old standby. "Hi."

She shifted closer, playing with the zipper on her brand new jacket. "Are you Santa Claus?"

He took in the signs: the not clean hair, the clothing that was still creased from its packing, the wary look in her eyes. This girl was part of Daniela's project. He sighed sadly. No wonder she'd been so determined to help.

The girl took another stepped forward. "My brother said Santa was the one who brung us food and presents."

He was more like the Grinch, actually, about to take their home away. "I'm not Santa, but I know who your Santa is."

Her eyes widened. "Can you tell him thank you? And can you tell him the cinnamon bread is my favorite?"

"I will." If Santa ever spoke to him again.

"Maybe Santa will bring us a new home too." She looked up at him. "We used to have a nice apartment, but then Mama got fired because I was sick and no one wanted her so we had to move here. But I don't like it. But we gots to go now, because they're going to knock the walls down."

"That sounds awful," he managed to say.

"My brother Jimmy says he'll take care of me, no matter what." Her thin chest puffed out. "He will too."

His heart cracked. Eddie had done the same for him. "I'm sure he will."

She head popped up, hearing something he wasn't attuned too. "I gots to go."

He watched her scurry into the cold building he was planning to tear down.

For someone with big brains, you got no sense, little bro.

"No kidding." Nico got up and walked to his car, hearing Eddie's mocking laughter in the wind.

Chapter Twenty-six

Under normal circumstances, if Daniela received a call in the middle of the night, she'd have been irritated beyond belief. It wasn't so irritating, though, when she couldn't fall asleep, which was the case since she'd left Nico and moved back into her own house.

Sighing, she fumbled around the nightstand for her phone. The number on the screen was long and foreign. Frowning, she deliberated a moment before she answered. "Hello?"

"Merry Christmas, sweetheart!" her father's voice boomed across the static-y connection.

"Daddy." She sat up and turned the light on. "Where are you?"

"We decided we needed some warmth, so we flew to Australia for the holidays. Sidney. But tomorrow we're headed to the Great Barrier Reef. What's this we hear about you firing Tony?"

The bastard tattled on her. She clenched the covers in her fist. "He started it. He's being a jerk."

"Hold on. Your mother wants to say hi." There was more static, and then her mother's voice came on. "We miss you, honey. How are you?"

She heard the real, underlying question and she sighed. "I miss Nonna."

"I know, honey. I'm sorry we aren't there, but Tony said he's in San Francisco with you."

"Unfortunately."

Her mother chuckled. "I remember when you and your brother were younger, and he'd do something that'd infuriate you, and you'd retaliate by taking something of his and holding it hostage. Some things don't change."

"I'm not holding anything hostage," she exclaimed, indignant.

"Aren't you?" Before she could answer, her mom said, "Tony means well, but he's a man, so he's going to be clueless sometimes."

Daniela smiled faintly when she heard her father's muffled protest.

"But even if he is clueless and deserves being punished for saying thoughtless things, which is what I imagined happened, Tony has your best interests at heart. Don't shut him out, honey. He's trying to help you."

She crossed her arms tight. "You don't know how thoughtless he's been."

"I doubt he does either," her mom said lightly. "You should tell him. We love you, Dani. Be happy."

Her dad called out his goodbye in the background, and then the line disconnected.

Daniela sat in bed, staring at the wall.

Her mother was right.

Pushing the covers aside, she left her room and headed to Tony's and pounded her fist on the door. "Tony, I need to talk to you," she yelled through the door.

He swung open the door, rubbing his eyes, wearing only pajama bottoms.

Crossing her arms, she leaned in the doorway. "How retro of you."

"Do you know what time it is?" he rasped in his sleep-husky voice.

"It's time to end this, according to Mom." She put her hands on her hips. "I noticed that you told on me, by the way."

"I didn't tell on you. Our parents asked how you were, and I said bitchy." He frowned at her. "Finish harassing me so I can go back to bed."

"You're a jerk."

He rolled his eyes. "So you've told me."

"I'm sick of you being my manager. I don't want a manager if that's how you're going to be." She hugged herself, willing herself to keep it together. "I want my brother back, the guy who was my best friend, who would have sent me a goofy card for my birthday, not have his secretary send me flowers."

He gazed at her, his brow furrowed.

She pointed at him. "Don't be a guy."

"The last time I looked in my pants, that's what I was."

"I mean listen to what I'm saying. I'm telling you I miss you. Since Nonna died, you've abandoned me." Tears filled her eyes and slipped silently down her face.

"Aw, hell, Dani, *don't cry*." He reached out and pulled her against him, holding her tight. "Yell at me. Throw things at my head. But I can't stand it when you cry."

"I'm sad." She sniffled. "You've been treating me

like I'm a client, but I'm not. I'm special, damn it."

"Yes, you are."

She looked up, glaring at him. "Are you laughing at me?"

"A little." He wiped the tears from her cheeks with his thumbs. "I'm sorry, Dani. I didn't mean to make you sad."

"Jerk." But she already felt better—lighter.

"I only want what's best for you, though, and you're making it difficult for me. I've been thinking about your soup kitchen."

Retracting, she looked at him warily. "What?"

"I'll help support your project, but on one condition. That you have someone manage the charity and you continue baking at least part-time." He crossed his arms and gazed at her steadily. "Before you get all bent out of shape, hear me out. You *love* baking. It's the core of you. You can't give it up, I just don't believe that'd make you happy. Think of what Nonna would say if you told her you were going to stop."

Nonna's voice popped in her head. *You must be hungry to speak such nonsense, Dani. Sit. We'll eat penne a la arrabiata and then make tiramisu, okay, bella?*

Tony tugged on one of her curls. "She wouldn't

let you quit either. But you can have both."

She shook her head, deflating. "It doesn't matter. The building I wanted got taken out from under me."

"We'll find another building."

"There's nothing in the city that's affordable."

"Are you questioning my ability to make this happen?"

A smile flirted with her lips. "God forbid."

"Smart ass." He pushed her toward the door. "Get out of here. I need my beauty sleep."

"Yes, you do." She grinned as a pillow hit her in the back on her way out. She returned to her room and snuggled in her bed, feeling a little better. Maybe she'd make *bocconotti* for Tony in the morning, since it was his favorite, and he was hers.

Chapter Twenty-seven

With her head resting directly on top of the bar at Grounds for Thought, Marley could feel the vibrations from the espresso machine reverberate through her brain. She hoped it'd shake some sort of idea into her, but so far it hadn't done anything but give her a headache.

Valentine patted her shoulder. "You should have taken my matchmaking abilities more seriously. I'm always right about these things."

"You're not helping," she mumbled against her arm.

"What?"

She lifted her head and frowned at her friend. "I have plenty of guilt on my own right now. I don't need more."

Valentine smiled sheepishly. "Sorry."

"I need help figuring out how to win Brian Benedict back."

She shook her head. "That's not going to be easy. You're not his favorite person right now."

"You've talked to him?" Marley grabbed her arm. "Where is he? I've tried calling but his phone is off. I've even tried going to his apartment but he doesn't seem to be there."

"He went away to Mexico for a few days."

A sick feeling churned in her stomach, and she couldn't help asking, "By himself?"

"Of course, by himself." Valentine rolled her eyes. "Although it'd serve you right if he had a rebound fling. He's a great guy, and you took him for granted."

"Rub it in, why don't you?"

"Well, you don't seem to hear otherwise." She took a sip of her tea. "I gave you the perfect guy and you didn't treat him like the gift he was."

"I know that. I'm kicking myself about it every second I'm awake and even in my sleep." Marley faced her friend. "Tell me the truth. Is it too late to try and get him back?"

Valentine studied her for a long, silent moment. Whatever she saw must have passed the test, because she shook her head. "I don't know. Brian said he needed a change of scenery to think things through. He's coming back in a couple days."

Panic spread icy through her veins. "What's he thinking through?"

The matchmaker threw her hands in the air. "I don't know. Whatever stuff guys need to work out."

"I've got to do something."

Valentine rested a hand on her arm. "You really like him?"

"I hadn't realized how much until I'd screwed it all up."

"Are you willing to do whatever it takes? Even if you have to beg?"

"Yes. I love him," she said without hesitation, and the words felt so true and real that she wanted to smack herself on her head for not realizing sooner.

"Okay." Valentine nodded, her demeanor all business as she pulled out her phone. She swiped the screen a couple times. "He comes back in two days. I'm supposed to pick him up at the airport, but you're going in my stead."

Marley worried her lip, thinking of all the things that could go wrong. "What if he doesn't want to go with me?"

"That's not an option. Failure isn't one of the choices here. You need to make him see reason."

"I can't make him love me."

"You don't have to." The matchmaker slid off the stool and tugged her skirt down. "Come with me. We need to arm you for battle."

She obediently got off her seat. "Why are you helping me?"

"Because I'm a love advocate." She marched out the door, a skinny redhead on the charge.

Just as Valentine was about to exit, the Hulk stepped into the doorway, blocking it with his width. He glared at her like she was a gnat harassing him.

Valentine, who looked tiny compared to him, just glared back. "You're in my way."

Marley thought he was going to growl—maybe even bite the woman in two. But he surprised her by stepping aside.

"I can help." Valentine handed him a card. "Call me," she ordered as she primly walked by, her purse swinging in the crook of her elbow.

Marley followed before the Hulk decided to take it out on her. "That was impressive," she said to her friend under her breath.

"I'm going to match him up." There was a determined light in her eyes.

"I believe you." Marley strode after her. "How did you have that card ready so quickly? Do you have some stashed in your bra?"

Valentine gasped. "A bra with a built-in card holder. That's brilliant. I may have to work on that."

"Valentine, where are we going?"

"Here." She swept into Romantic Notions, the posh lingerie store, and walked right up to the young woman manning the counter. "Nicole, we need something saucy to wear. For her."

Both women turned to inspect Marley.

She wanted to duck under their calculating gazes, which she equated to being much like Superman's laser vision.

"How saucy are we talking?" Nicole asked.

"Garters," Valentine said decisively. "Stockings."

"Stockings?" Marley gulped. "I don't—"

"Really saucy then." Nicole rubbed her hands together gleefully. "We can do that."

The two women discussed her like she wasn't there. They picked out some things, debated color, and then settled on a lacy garter and black stockings, with a matching bra.

Marley held up the bra, which seemed to be missing essential parts and pieces. "This has no cups."

"I know." Nicole winked wickedly at her. "He's going to love it."

"Where are the panties?"

"No panties," Valentine said.

She shook her head. "I can't *not* wear panties."

Valentine narrowed her eyes. "You can when the stakes are so high."

Could she go without underwear? She tried to picture it.

"Look at it this way," her friend said. "If it ensured you being loved for the rest of your life, would you take the risk?"

Marley turned to Nicole. "No panties, please."

Marley teetered on the heels she wasn't used to wearing as she moved out of the way of a large family with a hundred suitcases. One of the children eyed her. Could the kid see that she was naked underneath the trench coat?

Well, she wasn't completely naked. After all, she

was wearing the peek-a-boo bra, the garters, and the stockings. Otherwise she had nothing on but the expensive lotion Daniela had given her for her last birthday.

Still, just in case, she cinched the belt of her coat tighter.

To distract herself from her nerves, she pictured herself getting arrested by the airport police. She looked around, wondering if she looked like a hooker, standing against the column, waiting. She imagined being put in handcuffs and frisked.

She imagined Brian Benedict frisking her.

She fanned herself with her hand and then lifted all her hair off her neck. It was hot in this coat.

A wave of people poured out from the terminal. Marley stood up straight. Was this part of his flight? The monitor said it landed ten minutes ago.

She surveyed each passenger, looking for the right one. Just when she'd given up hope, she saw him striding through the security checkpoint.

He looked familiar but different—more tanned, his hair disheveled. He wore sandals and cargo shorts, with a long-sleeved dress shirt, sleeves rolled up, of course. His bag was slung on a shoulder, a baseball cap in the other hand.

Something inside her eased when she saw him. For the first time in days she had hope that this would turn out right.

Then he saw her, and he slowed as though he was reluctant to meet her.

No. She shook her head, tightening the belt one more time. She set her sights on him and went to meet him halfway.

She cleared her throat. "Welcome home."

"This is unexpected," he said, shifting his bag higher on his shoulder. He stopped directly in front of her. "Or are you on your way to a flashers' convention?"

She flushed, making sure the belt was still securely fastened. "Actually, I came to take you home."

Brian didn't say anything, just gazing at her like he was trying to figure her out. Then he shook his head. "I can take a cab."

"No, you can't." She stood straight, ignoring that she wobbled in the spiked heels. "Wonder Woman wouldn't let her man escape."

"Does that mean you have a red, white, and blue unitard under that trench?"

Taking a deep breath, she stepped right up to him, so she was pressed against the front of his body. In her heels, she was almost as tall as he was, so he met her gaze dead on. "I'll show you what I don't have on under here as soon as you forgive me for being slow."

He settled his glasses up his nose. "I'm not sure which part of that statement I'm supposed to glom on to."

"The part where I asked you to forgive me." She took his free hand, realizing she hadn't *really* understood how much she'd missed him until this moment. "I was so focused on the idea of what I thought I wanted, I didn't see what was in front of me until it was too late."

"What's in front of you?"

"A friend and confidante. A partner in crime." She squeezed his hand. "A lover."

"Those are my words."

"You were right. I'm not good with words, and you said it best. But they say a picture is worth a thousand words, so..." She reached into her purse and pulled out a framed photo.

He put his baseball cap on his head and took the picture. She watched his face, trying to measure how he'd feel seeing physical evidence of their love in the kiss on the pier.

Brian's expression didn't change.

Swallowing thickly, Marley said, "We looked happy. I *was* happy. I hate that I messed that up. But now that I know what I want, I'm not going to back down. I should warn you that I'll resort to anything, even not wearing panties, to get you back."

She thought his lips twitched, but she must have imagined it. "You said you didn't see what was in front of you until it was too late," he said.

"I know," she all but wailed.

He brushed her hair back. "It's not too late."

"Good." She reached up and pulled his mouth to hers. A sigh of relief went through her body the moment their lips touched. She pressed her heart to his, hoping he could hear that it beat for him.

Dropping his bag, Brian pulled her to him, squeezing her tight against him. "I was miserable this past week. The kind of miserable where I drank myself silly, only not even that helped."

She remembered the hangover she'd had after her night of drunken debauchery with Daniela and winced. "Me too."

Sweet on You

"I was really angry with you."

"I was, too." She whispered in his ear. "But I'm going to make it up to you."

"I hope however you do it includes what you haven't got on under this coat." He tugged lightly at her belt.

"It's not much," she said with a big smile. "Want to see?"

"Yes, please." He picked up his bag, not letting go of her hand. "I hate that I have to wait till we return home."

She shook her head. "I planned ahead. I brought Daniela's delivery truck, and I parked it on the top floor of the parking lot, away from all the other cars."

Brian's grin was slow but full. "Then lead the way, Super Marley."

"Super Marley. I like that." She pictured herself in boots instead of the uncomfortable spiked heels. With a cape, of course. "What's my superpower?"

"Love," he said, squeezing her hand.

She nodded as they walked out of the terminal. "I think you may be right."

Chapter Twenty-eight

*D*ANIELA CURLED UP on a couch, huddled in a blanket, staring at her brother. He sat in one of the oversized chairs, his feet propped on an ottoman. On his lap, he balanced his laptop, on which he was focused intently.

He'd decided to stay until Christmas. That gave her a few days with him, just the two of them. They'd agreed not to discuss work things until after the holidays, when he'd help her formulate a plan for going ahead with her charity idea.

She pursed her lips, imagining living in this big house alone. Well, not really alone, because she told Marley to stay even though she was going to strike out on her own. She liked having Marley there, though she suspected that the young woman would be moving in with her new boyfriend sooner as opposed to later.

The word *boyfriend* made her want to pout. Not that Daniela wanted a boyfriend. She wanted Nico, and Nico was definitely not a boy.

Tony closed his laptop and stared at her. "What's wrong?"

"What do you mean?" she said, burrowing deeper in her blanket.

"You're fidgety. That actually isn't unusual since you haven't stood still since you were born, but the forlorn sighing has to go."

"I'm not sighing forlornly."

He rolled his eyes. "You want me to go break his legs and take care of it once and for all?"

She couldn't help smiling. "You're such a Guido sometimes."

"I just care about you."

Tears popped into her eyes. "I'm going to miss you when you leave."

"I'm not gone yet." He set his laptop aside. "And I wanted to talk to you about that. What if I stayed?"

She sat up. "You're thinking of staying?"

He nodded. "Most of my clients are in Los Angeles these days, and it's a closer hop to LA from here. I like San Francisco, and I'll be closer to you."

"To keep tabs on me?"

"To spend more time with you," he corrected. "You were right. My priorities have been out of whack. I need to change that. You're here, and Mom and Dad are travelling all over the world. There's nothing keeping me in New York."

"But—" Her phone rang, and it was Eve. "Hold on while I take this."

She'd barely said hello when Eve exclaimed, "Congratulations, Daniela! I didn't think you were going to do it."

"Do it?" she asked, confused.

"Finish your store. The decorations look great from what I can see through the window."

"Decorations?" Frowning, she pushed the blanket aside. "Where are there decorations?"

"Inside your showroom."

"There shouldn't be anything inside my showroom but unused two-by-fours." She glanced at her brother, who was already putting on his shoes. "You're sure it's my space?"

"Of course." Eve paused. "You didn't do it?"

"No." She rooted around the floor for her slippers. "I'll be right down."

She hung up as Tony tossed her a sweater. "Let's go," he said. "We'll drive."

It was only a few blocks away, but she didn't argue with him this time. They rushed to the shop and double-parked right outside.

Eve stood in the doorway, cuddled warmly in the arms of a large, dark-haired man Daniela recognized as her friend's new husband.

"Treat and I were on our way home and I noticed it," Eve said as Daniela and Tony joined them.

"You were working this late?" Daniela asked.

Even in the dark, she could see Eve's blush. The blonde tucked her hair behind her ear. "Treat came to pick me up and we had some dessert before leaving."

A wave of longing swept over her. She and Nico used to have "dessert" all the time. Before the sadness overwhelmed her, she focused on her store. "I haven't had the lights installed in the front," she told Tony.

"Then why is it all lit?" he asked, taking his duplicate keys out and heading to the door. She tried to go around him to get in, but he pushed her back. "Let me check it out first, just in case."

She rolled her eyes, but arguing would have just delayed things. So she stayed back, tapping her foot impatiently.

"I'll go with you," Eve's husband said, following Tony inside.

"They're so annoyingly macho sometimes," Eve said, moving to her side. "I doubt there's a bad guy in there. What bad guy would leave behind a Christmas tree and lights?"

Daniela shook her head. "I'm baffled."

"You really didn't have it done?"

"I haven't even decorated at home."

Treat poked his head out the door. "Coast is clear."

Daniela's breath caught the moment she stepped inside. It looked like a winter wonderland. Garlands decorated the walls, wrapped in twinkling white lights. Reindeer stood in a cluster to one side, and stockings hung from one wall. In the center of the room, a huge tree glittered with ornaments and lights. Under the tree, there was one present, large and obvious.

Daniela looked around the room, in shock. It was like Nonna used to do — crazy and over the top. She inhaled the scent of Christmas, of pine and spice, and she could almost feel her grandmother standing next to her, grinning in delight.

"It looks like a Christmas store exploded in here," Treat said.

"It looks like our grandmother's home." Tony shook his head, a smile flirting with his lips. "She got a little crazy around the holidays."

Eve took Treat's hand. "We'll get out of your way, since everything looks okay. Call me tomorrow, Daniela. I want to hear everything."

Daniela bussed her friend's cheek. "Thank you."

Grinning, Eve shrugged. "I should thank you. This is going to make for a good story for my patrons tomorrow. Talk to you later."

Hands on her hips, she turned around and surveyed the room again. Amazing. "Did you do this?"

"No, but I wish I had. It's brilliant." He checked the tag on the present. "It's for you, of course."

"Check the stocking, your coal is probably in there," she said as she headed to it.

"Ha ha." He stared at the package. "What do you think it is?"

"I don't know." She picked it up. It was surprisingly light, like there was nothing inside. She shook it but nothing happened.

"Well, we know it's not a puppy," her brother said.

"Open it."

She sat on the floor and tore open the wrapping. There was endless tissue inside. When she reached the bottom of the box, there was a thick envelope. She opened it. "It's a legal document," she said with a frown.

"Is someone suing you for Christmas?" Her brother looked over her shoulder.

"No, it seems like someone is giving me a building," she said slowly, flipping through the pages.

"Let me see." He reached to take the document from her.

She held it out of his reach, scowling at him.

He grinned sheepishly. "Sorry. Habit. May I see it?" he asked sweetly.

She handed it over to him and began to pace. Maybe she read it wrong, but it seemed like Nico signed over the building to her. How?

Why?

"It seems Nico Cruz gave you a building for Christmas." Tony glanced up at her over the edge of the papers. "Cruz is the man you told me about?"

In a moment of weakness, she'd told her brother what had happened between her and Nico. He'd gotten so worked up, she'd had to sit on him to keep him from going to break Nico's legs. "That depends. Have you bought a firearm like you threatened?"

"Not yet, but there's still time." He handed her the papers. "He obviously cares about you, a lot, if he's just outright giving you the building he stole out from under you."

She stood up and studied all the decorations incredulously.

"Obviously you told him about Nonna's obsession with the holidays," her brother said as if reading her mind.

"Yes, but why would he bother to recreate it all? I don't get it. This took time."

"Are you sure you don't get it? Because it seems pretty clear to me. He cares about you. No man would go through this trouble, plus deed an expensive building to you, if you weren't important to him."

"I know!" she exclaimed. "That's what I don't get."

Tony shook his head. "You were never good at chess."

She stopped and glared at her brother. "What does that mean?"

"It means his move was to make amends in the only way he could. The next move is yours."

Sweet on You

"Really?" Frowning, she considered it. What Tony said felt right though. "What play do I make?"

"Do you want to capture the king or not?"

She thought she was done with him, but she'd lied to herself. She looked around the room, everything he'd done with such care and thought. She saw the details that she'd told him about Christmas at Nonna's that he'd replicated and her heart melted all over again. "I want the king."

"I don't need to wish you luck." Tony took her by the arms and kissed her forehead. "You always make what you want happen."

She threw her arms around him. "I love you, Tony."

"Which is why I know you won't deny me the opportunity to threaten this Cruz guy with bodily harm if he does anything stupid ever again."

"I'm not sure that's in the job description for a business manager."

"No, but it is for a brother." He smiled at her. "So, can I give you a ride somewhere? My car's outside."

Tony dropped her off at the Mandarin Oriental. She made him drive fast, not because she was nervous and wanted to get it over with but because she was impatient.

She wanted Nico. She wanted to kiss him and to cook for him. Most of all, she wanted to love him.

After she made him grovel for what he'd done, of course.

She strode through the lobby, not caring that she looked a sight in her pajama bottoms, slippers, and sweater. She went to the front desk and looked the girl behind the counter in the eye. "I'm here to see Nico Cruz."

"Is he expecting you?"

"Yes," she said confidently, knowing without a doubt that Nico was waiting for her. He might not suspect that she was going to come at—she looked at the time—10:32 at night, but he knew she'd have to come see him.

It was the point of his gift.

She waited impatiently as the front desk girl made a call. A murmured conversation, and then the girl waved to a guard. "Please swipe this lady to the penthouse."

"Thank you," Daniela said, following the guard.

The man gave her a discreet look, a smile hovering at the corners of his mouth.

She smiled. "I'm dressed to kill."

"You stopped *my* heart," he said with a wink as the elevator doors closed.

She tapped her foot as the elevator zipped up the building to the top floor. She arrived with a soft ping, and the doors glided open.

Nico stood waiting for her at the edge of the living room. To someone who didn't know him, he'd have looked casual. Untucked dress shirt with rolled up sleeves. Hands in his jeans' pockets. Bare feet.

But she knew him, and she recognized that he was taut. His jaw clenched tight, as if wanting to let her speak first. His gaze rested on her intently, and he stood still as if he didn't want to scare her away. She had no doubt that he'd stuffed his hands in his pockets to keep from grabbing her.

It made her feel powerful.

It made her want to soothe him.

"That's my second favorite outfit of yours." She nodded at him as she stepped out of the elevator.

He glanced down at himself. "This?"

She nodded. "My third favorite is you in a tux, and my all-time is you completely naked."

He watched her approach, his gaze guarded. "I hope you're implying you might like to see me naked again at some point."

"I'm not implying anything." Letting him puzzle that out, she stopped in front of him. "You've been busy."

"I had to make up for lost time."

"I don't understand why you did it." She took the documents out of her pocket and waved them. "This is obviously important to you."

"Yes." He held out his hand. "Sit with me and I'll explain."

There was no question, no thought—she took his hand and sat next to him.

"My mother left when I was twelve, leaving me with my older brother, who was barely more than a child himself," he began after a moment. "He got us a little room in an old, rundown motel. He hated it. He used to talk about tearing down the building so no one would have to live in that sort of squalor."

"The Harrison building," she said with dawning comprehension.

"I always thought it was both tragic and ironic that Eddie ended up dying there. The gang he'd been trying to evade dumped his body on the sidewalk out front." Nico faced her. "I promised Eddie that day I'd see the building destroyed. But some promises need to be broken. Eddie would have wanted it this way."

She gripped his hand, tears flowing down her cheeks, feeling the pain he was obviously feeling. She knew he spoke about both the past and the present, and her heart broke for him. She wanted to take him in her eyes and tell him he could tear down the building and put up a parking lot for all she cared.

But that wasn't what he needed, she realized. If he'd needed it, he'd have done it. He needed *her*.

The clarity was so sudden she almost expected to hear a chorus of angels. She shook her head. She should have realized it sooner. "You need me," she repeated out loud.

"Yes." He started to reach out to her face, but he pulled back. "I should have realized it sooner. I'm sorry I didn't. I'm especially sorry I hurt you."

"I didn't think men apologized."

"We do when it benefits us, and I have ulterior motives."

She moved closer, so she smelled the laundry fresh scent of his clothing and the spiciness she knew was all him. "What sort?"

He took her hand. "I have a business proposition to discuss with you. A merger."

"That sounds serious."

"It is. It's irrevocable." He tugged her onto his lap. "Once you agree, there's no going back."

"What are the terms?"

"Forever. Non-negotiable."

She looked around the grand hotel suite. "We may have to relocate the headquarters. I have a lot of pans."

"We can discuss that."

"And we need to discuss whether we want to expand."

He blinked, as though surprised by the thought. Then he said, in a voice full of emotion. "I'm in favor of expansion."

She pictured a little Nico sitting on the kitchen counter as she baked. She pressed a hand to her heart, the image filled it so fully. "I'd want rapid and aggressive expansion."

"I believe in going all out." He lifted her chin with his free hand. "But I have a couple more conditions of my own."

"I'm open to hearing them now."

"You have to leave your makeup all over the counter of my bathroom."

"*Our* bathroom," she corrected.

He smiled, but then he became all business again. "You're required to deposit underwear all over our headquarters."

She sighed dramatically. "I suppose I can arrange that."

"And you have to wear an apron when you bake. *Only* an apron."

"You drive a hard bargain." She slipped her arms around his neck. "But I think I can deal."

"Good."

She pressed her lips to his. It was reverent and slow, still spicy, but an element of care, as if they were both savoring the feeling.

Then he grabbed her closer, and it heated up.

He leaned backwards, until he reclined with her on top. She sat up and yanked her sweater off. "I thought of wrapping myself in a ribbon."

He watched her lift her shirt over her head. "You're a gift, regardless of how you're decked out."

Pausing, she looked at him, knowing she probably looked sappy. "I didn't thank you for my present," she said as she began to unbutton his shirt.

He shook his head, lifting up so she could push his shirt off him. "That was yours to begin with. I just returned it to the rightful owner. Before you say anything more, I know I'm doing the right thing. My brother knows it, too, I think."

She kissed him, her heart overflowing. She felt his hand snake under her pajama bottoms and she reached between them to undo his jeans.

They disengaged to discard the rest of their clothing and then clasped each other again, skin against skin, heartbeat against heartbeat.

Nico nuzzled her neck. "I wasn't sure I was ever going to get the pleasure of this again. I fucked up."

"You did." She arched her back to give him more targets. "Big time."

"Don't mince words," he said as he kissed his way down her torso to her breasts. Then he gazed into her eyes, cupping her face. "I couldn't decide what I missed more, your lovely face or the sweet smell of home you've given me."

Her heart expanded with love. "I'd have thought it'd be my body."

Sweet on You

He grinned wickedly. "Maybe I was wrong."

"Don't worry." She lowered her mouth down to his. "I'll set you right."

Their embrace was one part him, an equal part her, liberally laced with passion, an extra serving of love, and a pinch of fairy dust. She saw sparks, fireworks, and rockets.

She felt his hands all over her, as though reclaiming lost territory. She pressed herself close, humming in need as his erection pulsed against her hip.

His hands speared into her hair, and he tugged her head back. "Condom?"

She swallowed, and then she shook her head. "Unless you aren't sure."

"Baby, I'm all in." He kissed her like she was treasure. As he slid into her, he brushed her hair from her eyes. "You're mine, Daniela."

She heard the future in his rough voice. She heard the passion and so much love that her heart overflowed. She squeezed him close. "I love you, too."

He thrust all the way into her, and she moaned. He paused there, his eyes squeezed shut.

So she took the reigns. She swiveled her hips,

deep, faster and faster until they were sweaty. The couch squeaked, and her legs stuck to the surface. But she barely noticed—her entire focus was on Nico lying under her, the taut column of his neck as he struggled not to come, the desperate grip of his hands on her hips, the hard pulse of him inside her.

She could feel him escalate, and that brought her closer. "I can't hold out."

"Then come," he whispered darkly against her neck, driving into her.

She cried out just as he did. He stiffened under her as she undulated over him, wringing every last bit of pleasure from him.

She collapsed on top of him. "Checkmate," she whispered triumphantly.

Nico held her closer. "We both won."

She nodded, kissed his shoulder, and then sighed happily as she felt him stir inside her. "And I think we're going to win again, very soon."

Epilogue

Nonna always said the recipe for the perfect Christmas morning was equal parts sweet and bitter, sprinkled with joy and served with hope.

Daniela stood in the window of the kitchen nook and stared at the sunshine streaking across the sky. The sweet was Tony, Marley, and all her new neighborhood friends. The bitter was her grandmother being gone and her parents all the way across the world.

Joy was Nico.

Hope was the future.

Nonna would say this was the perfect Christmas, and Daniela would have to agree.

There was the shuffling of feet. She turned as Nico strode in. His hair was sleep-rumpled, and he wore silk pajama bottoms and a T-shirt. She knew under the pajamas he was completely bare, and the thought made her grin devilishly.

"Your bathroom is atrocious, even in the dark," he said, walking up to her.

"The red velvet walls are unfortunate, but the bathtub rocks."

"I followed the leopard print carpet to the kitchen. It's like some sort of strange African yellow brick road." He wrapped his arms around her waist and kissed her lightly. "You're up early."

"Christmas breakfast. I'm making my grandmother's *pain perdu*." Nonna believed all things Italian were the best, but the French did know a thing or two, and their version of French toast was one of them.

"Is that what smells delicious?" Nico nuzzled her neck. "I thought it was you."

"I'm dessert." She slipped her hands under his shirt and sighed. "After presents, of course."

"I gave you your present last night," he whispered against her ear.

She held up her hand, a shiver of excitement shooting through her as she looked at the engagement ring. It was an art deco ring with a ruby, large and bold, surrounded on one side by a spray of sparkly white diamonds in all shapes and sizes. He told her it reminded him of her: fiery passion with a combination of old-fashioned and modern that he found enchanting.

"I still can't believe it," she said, shaking her head. "It's all so fast."

"I told you that when I find what I want, I get it, and I want you." He lifted her chin and looked into her eyes. "Forever."

Tony stumbled into the kitchen like a zombie. "Coffee," he moaned. "And please stop mauling each other in my presence."

She grinned at Nico before stepping away to get two coffee mugs out. She poured them each coffee, both black, and handed it to each of her men, who'd sat down at the large table. "You're going to have to get used to Nico mauling me, Tony. He asked me to marry him."

"I know."

"What do you mean, you know?" She frowned. "He only asked me last night."

"I talked to your brother first," Nico said, drawing her down onto his lap.

"Nico has old world sensibilities. Nonna would have approved." Tony sipped his coffee, closing his eyes in bliss. "You're good at cake, Dani, but at coffee you're the best. You're a lucky man, Nico."

Her fiancé smiled like the cat that ate the canary. "I know."

Marley entered the kitchen, bright-eyed and blushing, holding her new man's hand. She wore a silky dark blue robe with yellow Batman symbols that still had creases in it, and her hair was down.

The first time Daniela had seen Brian, she'd liked him instantly. She'd insisted he and Marley join their Christmas breakfast. Marley was family, after all, which made Brian family, too.

"Is Christmas breakfast soon?" Marley asked, taking a seat at the table. "I'm starved."

Tony narrowed his gaze at Brian, who still held the young woman's hand.

"The *pain perdu* will be ready in half an hour." Daniela put a restraining hand on her brother's shoulder as she refilled his cup. For some reason he bristled at Brian's presence. Maybe he was jealous, because Marley no longer looked at him with fawning adoration.

What he needed was his own woman. She'd talk to Marley's friend Valentine. Tony was going on forty—

maybe it was time to bring in the big guns.

Gleeful at the prospect of hiring a matchmaker for her brother, she clapped her hands once. "Passion fruit mimosa, anyone?"

Marley shuddered, but Brian settled his glasses more solidly on his nose as he nodded. "I'd love to try some."

"I knew I liked him." She winked at her former assistant as she pulled out a wine glass.

Nonna had always insisted Christmas was a celebration of family and life and deserved champagne, which she usually mixed with some sort of juice depending on her mood. Pomegranate when she wanted to bring in a more fertile year, bittersweet grapefruit when Nonni had passed away.

Daniela thought passion fruit was the perfect juice to add to the bubbles this year. She poured one for Brian, another for herself, and coffee for Marley. As she raised her glass to offer a toast, the doorbell rang.

She and Tony frowned at each other. "It's barely dawn," he grumbled, getting up from the table. "Did you invite someone else over?"

"Not until later." Lola and Eve, plus their families,

were coming over for sweets in the afternoon. Olivia and her husband had been invited, too, but Eve had called last night to say Olivia wouldn't make it—she gave birth to a Christmas Eve baby boy, named Parker after her father.

She settled back onto Nico's lap, nestled happily in his arms. A shiver of anticipation shot through her as she thought about the day they'd have their own kids. A girl and a boy, who'd tease and harass and love each other their whole lives.

He kissed her, looking at her as if he could read her thoughts.

She bet he could. She sighed happily and took a sip of her mimosa. It was sweet, with enough tang and fizz to make it interesting.

"Holy cow." Marley grabbed her hand and gaped at the engagement ring. She turned to Brian and said, "Don't get me wrong. My Batman robe kicks ass, but so does that ring."

Daniela laughed, not able to resist winking at Brian. She knew he had another present for Marley as well—one that kicked ass *big time*. He rented Marley a studio for a year. Daniela had helped him pick it out. It had a brightly lit area but the back area was completely dark. Marley was going to love it.

Tony rushed into the kitchen, looking wild-eyed and more than a little harassed. Before she could ask what was going on, someone trailed in after him.

The woman was tall, wrapped head-to-toe in black. Blond hair peeked from the edges of the black cap pulled down low over her head. Her cheekbones jutted, making her look so gaunt Daniela had the urge to make a batch of *zeppoli* stuffed with sweetened ricotta to serve to her.

But it was her face that was most striking: the desperate look in her eyes and her makeup, which ran down her cheeks with her tears.

Something about her was very familiar. Daniela frowned, trying to place the woman. One of Tony's exes?

"Is her face melting?" Marley whispered to Brian.

Nico shifted under her. Mouth close to her ear, he whispered, "Isn't that —"

"This is Sophie Martineau," Tony said, raking a hand through his hair. "She just decided to stop by, I guess."

The woman swallowed a teary hiccup. "It's my birthday, and I want cake."

Daniela looked at her brother.

He shrugged helplessly.

She looked at the famous actress, recognizing her now under the clownish makeup. Nico kissed her shoulder and pushed her to standing and toward the woman. She smiled at him over her shoulder. He already knew her so well.

Then she turned her smile to the actress, hands outstretched. "We don't have cake today, but we have my grandmother's *pain perdu*, and I guarantee it's even better than my chocolate cake."

She took the woman's icy hands in her own and drew her to the table.

"Lost bread?" Sophie said in her trademark husky voice, which wavered this morning.

"Translated, yes. It's a sort of souffléed French toast." She pulled out a seat from the table and guided Sophie into it. "Sit. I'll get you a mimosa."

The woman nodded, looking dazed.

She went to the refrigerator and pulled out the champagne and juice. As she reached for a glass, Nico's arm snaked around her waist. He lowered his mouth to her ear. "Do I have a lifetime of taking in waifs and strays to look forward to?"

"Do you mind?"

Smiling, he pushed her hair from her face. "No, as long as you're there."

She looked at the table. "Two months ago, I'd never have imagined a Christmas morning like this."

"Me either." He kissed her. And then he kissed her again, holding her face in his hands like it was precious. "It's the sweetest Christmas ever."

Don't miss the rest of the Laurel Heights series!

Perfect For You #1
Close To You #2
Return To You #3
Looking For You #4
Dream Of You #5

Also fall in love with Kate Perry's sexful, playful novels of family and love including *Playing Doctor* and *Playing for Keeps*...

Playing Doctor

After catching her research partner-slash-fiancé with the intern, Dr. Daphne Donovan returns home to lick her wounds and figure out how to fix her life. It doesn't take a genius to figure it out: being an uber-brilliant Doogie Howser has made her life miserable while all the normal people she knows are happy and content.

There's only one thing to do: become normal. No more being the wunderkind of childhood disease research. All she wants is a regular nine to five job, two-point-five children, a white picket fence, and a blue collar husband.

Except normal isn't all it's cracked up to be, especially after she meets Ulysses Gray. Gray is everything she doesn't want: smart, incredibly handsome, and a doctor--just like her ex-fiancé. She wants to deny him--and herself--but she can't resist playing doctor...

Playing for Keeps

Since her mother's death more than fifteen years before, Grace Connors has been the matriarch of her family. She's put her own dreams on hold to raise her younger sisters and keep her ex-marine father in line.

So when her sister Nell decides to get married, it's on Grace to make it a wedding their mother would have been proud of. It can't be hard to organize a party, right?

But then everything falls apart, including her budding romance with her sexy best friend Pete.

Caught in the crossfire with the enemy at her back, will Grace be able to fix it all before she becomes a casualty of love?

Legend of Kate

Kate has tangoed at midnight with a man in blue furry chaps, dueled with flaming swords in the desert, and strutted on bar tops across the world and back. She's been kissed under the Eiffel Tower, had her butt pinched in Florence, and been serenaded in New Orleans. But she found Happy Ever After in San Francisco with her Magic Man.

Kate's the bestselling author of the Laurel Heights Novels, as well as the Family and Love and Guardians of Destiny series. She's been translated into several languages and is quite proud to say she's big in Slovenia. All her books are about strong, independent women who just want love.

Most days, you can find Kate in her favorite café, working on her latest novel. Sometimes she's wearing a tutu. She may or may not have a jeweled dagger strapped to her thigh...

Printed in Great Britain
by Amazon.co.uk, Ltd.,
Marston Gate.